WITH FEARFUL BRAVERY

WITH FEARFUL BRAVERY
Lynne Kositsky

The publisher gratefully acknowledges the support of the Canada Council for the Arts
and the Ontario Arts Council for its publishing program. We acknowledge the
financial support of the Government of Canada through the Canada Book Fund
(CBF) for our publishing activities, and the Government of Ontario through the
Ontario Media Development Corporation, an agency of the Ontario Ministry
of Culture, and the Ontario Book Publishing Tax Credit Program.

Library and Archives Canada Cataloguing in Publication

Kositsky, Lynne, author
With fearful bravery / Lynne Kositsky.

Issued in print and electronic formats.
ISBN 978-1-77086-409-2 (pbk.). — ISBN 978-1-77086-410-8 (html)

I. Title.

PS8571.²⁄₃85W58 2014   JC813'.54   C2014-905120-4
C2014-905121-2

Cover photo and design: Angel Guerra/Archetype
Interior text design: Tannice Goddard, Soul Oasis Networking
Printer: Trigraphik LBF

Printed and bound in Canada.

The interior of this book is printed on 30 % post-consumer waste recycled paper.

DANCING CAT BOOKS
AN IMPRINT OF CORMORANT BOOKS INC.
10 ST. MARY STREET, SUITE 615, TORONTO, ONTARIO, M4Y 1P9
www.cormorantbooks.com

*In memory of Hannelore Heinemann Headley,
who first introduced me to the history of Shanghai and its
acceptance of Jewish refugees before and
during the Second World War.*

1939

The Year of the Hare

CHAPTER 1

We are standing in the port of Genoa. Waves, battling the wind, climb high enough to splash around our feet, and spikes of rain lash our faces. I tug my too-small coat around me and fasten my little sister Lotty's jacket buttons, pulling her hood over her beacon-red hair. We are both shivering, partly from the cold, partly — at least in my case — from the frightening events that we might encounter on the way to Shanghai or in Shanghai itself.

"Heaven keep us from the Nazis," I murmur. If Tateh were here he would probably say that the weather's a bad omen. As it is, he's likely intoning Hebrew prayers for us in a prison camp somewhere in Germany. He'll do anything he can to keep our family safe, and has always believed that when praying he has a private line to God. But perhaps his faith, like mine, has been badly shaken, possibly shattered, by Hitler's obvious hatred of the Jews and his cruel practices. How could God allow Hitler to take aim against us? What unknown crimes have we committed?

After our desperate escape from Berlin in an overcrowded train, Mameh is attempting to exchange the tickets we hold for the ship *Julio Cesare*, which arrives in a month, for a berth on the *Conte Biancamano*, now in port. They are both bound for Shanghai, but waiting four weeks for the *Cesare* might land us in trouble. There's no telling when the port of Shanghai will close to Jewish refugees. There are four of us: Mameh, Lotty (three years old but still sucking her thumb), a friendly old woman named Frau Gold, and me.

With one eye closed in a perpetual wink and a face like a wrinkled apple, Frau Gold has shared our train carriage since Berlin and is happy to continue on with us, as she has no relatives left alive in the world. Lotty calls her New Oma, as our real grandmothers have both died. I've begun to call her that too. I'm Freda, aged eleven, but very grown-up for my age, as my *tateh* used to say. I'm the older sister of Lotty and general manager of all the odds and ends of life when Mameh's missing or distracted, which happens more often than one might suppose.

New Oma is the only one of us who has tickets for the boat now docked. Mameh seems most anxious to have her accompany us as we approach the *Conte Biancamano*. I'm sure she's up to something. She's painted her face with vampire-red lipstick, black eye *maquillage* (as she calls it), and an application of glittery powder, which, star-like, floats across her cheekbones. She has a calculating look that I've seen many times before. Even though her lipstick is cracked like an old dish at the corners of her mouth, the black spikes of her eyelashes clumped together, she is about to charm someone. There's no point in wondering who he might be — it's always a he — but from past experience I know I'll discover it soon enough. She's a terrible embarrassment to me, and I wish I could be travelling with Tateh instead of Mameh. But Tateh's gone.

By the time we close in on the *Conte Biancamano*, I'm so out of breath I start to wheeze. Refugees press toward the captain, yelling about their need to get on board at all costs. Exhausted, I slump down on the damp wharf. Lotty slides down next to me, niggling when she feels wet sand and sharp stones under her backside.

"Stand up, girls, stand up," yells Mameh. "I need you to be in the crowd, pushing forward with the rest, so I don't lose my place if I can't slide through and reach the captain before everyone else." So that's what her *maquillage* is all about. And her high heels. And her silk stockings with their seams that looked straight when we set out from our train carriage but zigzag up her legs now: to charm the man in charge well enough to get us berths on the boat. But I'm not about to be left alone in the middle of the crowd. We almost lost her that way in Berlin. She had gone on before us, carrying all our documents and tickets. Lotty and I were stuck at the train checkpoint till she remembered we were supposed to be travelling with her and returned, somewhat grumpily, to show the Nazis our papers. I'm not going to be left behind again. So I lurch to my feet and do my best to follow her, dragging Lotty along by her jacket sleeve. I turn around to check New Oma is behind us. She is.

Mameh parts the refugees like Moses parted the Red Sea. They are only too pleased to draw back, to stare at her, to wonder what such a glamorous, sparkly woman is doing here among the frump brigade, the dingily dressed matrons and tieless men, their crowds of shabby children buzzing like bees around them. Even though her eyes are now so smudged that she looks like a raccoon, they must think she's famous, perhaps a star from Hollywood. The pathway clear, she glides her way over to the captain. The forward surge of the crowd as the ocean of bodies closes behind her crushes me between a rather large would-be passenger and a member of the crew. "Dear *signor*," I hear Mameh say as I struggle to extricate myself, then push forward with Lotty to reach her. New Oma limps along behind us. We are caught up in the melee, a little boat on stormy seas, trying to move toward Mameh on imaginary waves.

"Dear *signor*, if I could just have your attention for a moment?" she begs the captain in that helpless-sounding way she has, hiking her skirt above the knee and straightening her stocking seams in front of him. Tacky indeed, but she is having the desired effect. His eyes widen. He can't stop staring at her legs. Pulling our tickets from her bag, she takes the opportunity to shove them into his hand.

"Forgive my importuning you, *signor*. But we have been travelling with my mother. Here she comes now. She has a ticket for your ship, the *Conte Biancamano*. Unfortunately I could only obtain tickets for the children and myself on the *Julio Cesare*, though we so wish to be with the children's oma. Our husbands were arrested by the Nazis and are probably dead, leaving us alone in the world. Is there anything you could do for us?"

"As you can see, dear *signora*, I'm besieged with requests. Everyone wants exactly what you want, and my ship is already crammed. I'm carrying double my usual number of passengers." His eyes travel up to her bust, and then to her blonde curls, or coiffure, as she calls her hairdo. He can't look away.

"Please, oh please, kindly *Capitano*." Mameh brushes a tear from her mascaraed eye. "I'm a weak woman, and need to sail on the same ship as my mother so she can help take care of my daughters and I can help take care of her. And besides, we don't have anywhere to stay till the *Julio Cesare* comes in." She puckers her lips. "Please — *per favore* — *signor*. You don't know how much it means to me ... to us."

"Hmm. I suppose I could ask a number of the crew to vacate their cabin and sleep on deck so you could stay there, but it would definitely be fourth — uh, D class accommodation, which you're obviously not ..."

"That would be wonderful." Mameh smiles her best-high-super-spectacular smile. As her face lights up, the crowd, entranced by her story to the point of forgetting their own, smile too, although one woman shouts out that she doesn't mind going D class either, just as long as she can get on the boat. Now I understand at least one reason why Mameh wanted to remain friendly with New Oma: to help us sail on the earlier ship. Like me, she must be worried that Shanghai will soon close its borders to Jewish refugees trying to escape Hitler.

The men and women, the whimpering babies, the darkening sky, all close in on me. It's beginning to rain harder, wet patterns decorating the ground and looping together to make puddles. My feet in my outgrown boots are both agonizing and soaking. But we are at last close to the gangway to the ship, thankfully hurrying away from a group of Nazi officers lounging around the harbour. Like some of the Nazis who ravaged our house in Berlin, the eyes of the officer closest to me are an extraordinary light blue. I fancy that if I could stand close enough to their owner to examine them, I would be able to see right through his irises to his brains, just as we'd been able to examine the cogs and wheels of the clocks Tateh brought home after his shop was barred on orders of Hitler. He opened the backs of them for me when he was in an unusually good mood, to show me how they worked. They whirred and clicked. Nazi brains probably consist of mechanical parts too.

"You are the queen of mothers, dear lady," the captain says, picking up our suitcase. "Please allow me to help you onto the ship. Be careful. The gangway's slippery, and people can be pushy." Of course, no one could be pushier than Mameh. But I keep my traitorous thoughts under lock and key.

"Thank you, dear *signor*," she smirks. "Say *grazie*, girls."

"*Grazie, signor*," I say obligingly. Noticing that Lotty has opened her mouth as wide as a baby bird's beak when it's waiting for a worm, I glare and shake my head at her. She's bound to ask something inappropriate, such as why are the captain's nails so filthy, or why does he have such a large lump on his neck? "Zip your lips," I hiss. Foiled, she shuts her mouth. In a minute we are on the ship, ready to sail to Shanghai, which, we've been assured by the captain, still accepts Jewish refugees.

CHAPTER 2

It's summer. I'm in the park playing tag with Tateh. It's my turn to tag him. I can run as fast as a deer, but he can run faster, and my legs begin to ache as the chase continues. I careen forward in a last desperate attempt to catch him. The gap between us grows ever wider until he slips out of the park and vanishes into a carmine haze as the sun begins to dip.

Where can he be? He knows I'm not allowed to go home by myself. I'm frightened to be on my own. Especially when it's changing from dusk to darkness. Perhaps he's playing a trick on me, circling around and re-entering the park behind my back, placing his fingers over my eyes and asking me to guess who he is. He wouldn't leave me here alone, would he?

"Tateh, come back," I cry desperately, searching behind every tree, staring up into nests of menacing branches. But he's become invisible, is quite, quite gone. As I turn, I see a big black and white sign on the grass: WARNING! JEWS AND DOGS NOT ALLOWED IN THE PARK. *A Nazi officer stands beside it. Tateh must have noticed the sign and soldier and gone to another country without me, a place where Jews can play tag without fear of punishment.*

The thought of losing him is unbearable. It's getting as dark and cold as a cellar. I don't know where to go. I'm not allowed to be in the park, but I'm not allowed to quit it by myself either. What shall I do? I begin to cry ...

My sobs turn into a cough as I start to wake up. I don't open my eyes. I'm keeping them shut, hoping for one last glimpse of Tateh. He appears for a second, translucent, lit by stars, before disappearing into the black inky pool of the past.

"I do wish you'd stop coughing, Freda," Mameh complains, her voice coarsened by sleep. "You've been barking like a dog for days, keeping us all from getting our beauty rest. You could control it if you wanted to, if you didn't feel the need to be so irritating."

I ignore her. After all, it's not as though I cough on purpose. I've tried to stifle it, but can't. A horrid tickle starts low in my throat before plummeting into my chest and causing a crashing pain. When I attempt to breathe in, I feel as if my lungs are full of mashed potatoes. Sometimes I panic. New Oma rubs me on the back till I can manage a halting breath.

The train has stopped its metallic clanking. Instead it's rocking from side to side like a baby's cradle. Rocking? How can that be? Trains don't rock. Now I remember: We've been travelling for weeks. We're on a ship, the *Conte Biancamano*. And close to Shanghai, the captain told us yesterday.

I open one eye. It feels sticky and painful. I close it again, sit up too fast, and bang my forehead hard on the ceiling. The ceiling? Perhaps the blow has damaged my brain. It's certainly given me a headache. But as my reopened eye adjusts to the dark — the other eye still shut — I can see I'm so close to the ceiling, it's a wonder I didn't knock my head off. I'm in one of the top bunks of a two-bunk cabin. Mameh, still nagging about my cough, is across from me, and Lotty lies in the lower bunk.

Someone's mattress must be beneath mine. It's New Oma's. She calls out to ask if I need a drink of water. Not wishing to disturb her sleep further, I refuse. But she's already gone to fetch it. I'm so pleased she's still travelling with us. Her presence provides us with the warmth and care we all too often don't get from Mameh. After a couple of mouthfuls of liquid, my coughing spasm subsides. I dive through reality and back into my dreams. A kaleidoscope of memories crashes through my brain, colliding with nightmarish flashes of Nazis and guns. Everything scrunches together as I dive backwards into the water of time.

Kristallnacht. There is a confusion of shouting and screaming in the streets, an acrid stench of burning, and the brutal noise of windows shattering. Houses and synagogues are set alight, and — as we soon find out — people murdered. It feels as if the whole world is on fire.

A man is thrown so forcefully against our living room window that he smashes the glass and ends up, dazed and bleeding, on our floor. He brings with him an aura of smoke and sweat and fear. We jump up, dismayed. The man's unwelcome, accidental presence in our home changes our lives with a chilly finality. The Nazis want to be rid of us.

I swim back to consciousness, suddenly recalling everything that has happened: How friends and neighbours lining up for bread were shot dead. How Tateh managed to bring his clocks home one night, after the Nazis closed his shop and threw him out of it. How the Nazis burst into our house and smashed all the clocks before dragging Tateh away. How I might never see him again. "Tateh, Tateh," I cry, desolate, my words once again bringing on a fresh paroxysm of coughing.

CHAPTER 3

The ship bumps, rocks, and rolls sideways. I'm resting in one of the lower bunks, but Lotty has disappeared, no doubt with New Oma shadowing her. I don't know where Mameh has gone, but assume that as usual she's socializing with the captain. I struggle out of bed, dress, and crawl up the stairs to the deck. The ship is idling in what one member of the crew assures us is the Whangpoo River, but another calls the Yangtze. What strange, funny names the river has! They conjure up visions of the colourful pantomimes Tateh used to take me to when I was little.

We're so close to the wharf that though it's foggy, I can see it over the railing I'm leaning on. New Oma lifts Lotty up so that she can see it too. "W-why can't we get off?" she wails. "I w-want to get off."

"You'll be very wet, *maidel*, if you get off here." New Oma's legs are buckling under my sister's weight. Lotty puts her thumb in her mouth and sucks it hard.

"You'll lose your thumb if you keep doing that," I say meanly. "It'll just turn blue and fall off. And so will your arm. And then where will you be?"

"N-no it won't fall off. If it did, I'd just s-stick it back on with g-glue anyway, you silly."

I don't know why I'm so nasty to my sister, but sometimes I can't stop myself, especially when Mameh is horrid to me or I'm worried. And I'm certainly worried now. Not to mention as sick as a dog that has swallowed his own tail. I lean over the rail again — this time to throw up — and catch a glimpse of a small boat heading toward us through the smoky mist.

"It's the doctor," the crewman tells us. "Stick out your tongues for inspection. He'll be here shortly. Only joking, young lady," he says to Lotty, who has removed her thumb from her mouth and is sticking her tongue out so far the crewman says he can see her tonsils, not to mention the Leaning Tower of Pisa. Everyone around us grins. One man guffaws as he musses her hair. Lotty is obviously a favourite with the other passengers but hates to be laughed at. She points a finger at the man. "No, n-no," she cries.

"Why don't you wave?" New Oma asks. "The doctor will like that." Lotty flaps her hand mechanically. She doesn't even seem to know what she's waving at. But small children, I've found, love to wave: at other small children, at squirrels on the fence, at household cats, even at nothing at all. Lotty is no exception.

A ladder is lowered for the doctor, who is followed up to the deck by a nurse in starched linens. I try to stifle my hacksaw of a cough, but it only makes me hack more. What if he realizes I'm sick and doesn't let me off the ship? What if he sends me back to Hitler in Germany? I'll be sent away like Tateh.

Mameh has joined us, wearing a floaty voile dress and high heels. Even though I can't see him, I imagine that the captain, who usually follows her every move, is watching her from the bridge. She's probably just left him. What he doesn't understand is that after the ship docks, she'll likely have no further use for him. He has given us delicious food and looked after her requirements for alcohol and cigarettes through the voyage, and that's enough for her.

"For the love of heaven," she says, "stop that braying, Freda, before the doctor reaches us. Sometimes I think you do it on purpose to draw attention to yourself. If you can't stop, hold your breath till the spasm passes."

"Yes, s-s-stop. You're giving me a headache."

"Your stuttering gives *me* a headache," I shoot back at Lotty. Cough.

A long line of refugees is forming, and the doctor jabs each of them in the arm — for what, I don't know. Like a game of Broken Telephone, the word *smallpox* passes from one refugee to another in the queue. Smallpox is a scary word, no question, but I hate needles, and the thought of being speared by one makes me feel worse than ever. I try not to breathe through my cotton wool lungs as the doctor moves closer, feel the cough building in my chest.

"We've got a sick one here and no mistake," the nurse calls out, her voice strident as the ship's foghorn. She's been marching up the line ahead of the doctor feeling heads and swabbing throats before halting directly in front of me. She presses two fingers to my forehead. I can't suppress my cough a moment longer. It flames up through my throat before exploding into the dirty air; I shiver from sickness and fear. "Hot head, red face. This girl's got a fever," the nurse booms to the doctor through the intervening rows of refugees. "A high fever." Her voice rattles my ears.

I cough again. Strange noises erupt from me. I sound like next-door's cat in Berlin, who yowled and screeched every night with his cat buddies.

Those closest to me scramble to get away. Some actually quit the deck. Others look unsure. Perhaps they're contemplating jumping over the rail and into the water.

"It's a nothing cough, nurse," says Mameh, trying to place herself between the nurse and me. She is unsuccessful. "A forced cough. She does this all the time at home. She just wants the attention. There's absolutely nothing wrong with her."

"I beg to differ. If I'm not very much mistaken, madam, your daughter has pneumonia. I cannot imagine why you allowed her to travel in this condition."

"We had no option. We had to escape Germany. My husband had already been arrested. Besides, my daughter was in perfect health when we set out."

This, for once, is true. But Mameh sounds cowed. She is no match for Dragon Woman, who stands in front of her, immovable as a cement block. The woman cannot be shifted by Mameh's wiles or pleading. Instead she opines in a loud hiss through her serpent teeth that it's a wonder I'm not dead.

"If you give the medicine for her, we can take her with us. Will look after her, no problem," says New Oma.

"Take her with you? To one of the filthy refugee *heims* you'll be housed in? It's too late for that."

New Oma shrivels into herself like a snail retreating into its shell. Dazed with fright though I am, I realize that Dragon Woman has been doing her best to save me. But as she's said, it's too late. I can't believe I've come all this way to avoid being killed by Hitler only to die in Shanghai. She bellows for the doctor again. I'm certain her voice can be heard all the way back to Genoa. I imagine a thousand people in Italy turning their heads toward the *Conte Biancamano*, hearing not her words but the tenor of them and wondering if a storm is coming in. As the doctor starts toward me, my thoughts twist together. *There's nothing anyone, nurse or doctor, can do to help. My illness is a risk to everyone. Now I'll be sent back to the Nazis for sure — before I infect everyone in China. I'll be imprisoned somewhere with mud and shit on the floor. And there I'll die.*

CHAPTER 4

The trip from the ship to the hospital is like another ghastly dream. There are trucks to collect the refugees as they disembark, but a cart is sent for me. Drawn by a Chinese man wearing a cone-shaped hat, it jounces and jerks over the cobbles. The crooked streets exhale strange and exotic perfumes together with the stink of garbage, and through the slats of the cart I can't help notice there is a dead Chinese man abandoned on the road. What did he die of, and how come no one had picked him up and buried him? Shanghai is as alien to me as another planet, and tears are leaching down my cheeks. I'm shocked at the sights and foreign stench of the city, can't help but feel pleased when we finally reach the hospital, forbidding though it looks

I still panic every time I see a hypodermic needle, but become more comfortable when I realize the Dragon Woman has disappeared, must still be working on other incoming ships. The doctor who's looked after my case since I arrived has kind eyes and a gentle manner.

"You have pneumonia, Freda. It's very serious indeed." He pats my hand. "It probably started with a mild infection such as a chest cold and grew worse during your journey. Do you understand?"

I nod.

"I know you hate needles, but you must continue to take them if you're to get completely better. They contain a new remedy." He adjusts his spectacles, the bridge of which is far too big for his small nose. He also adjusts his skullcap — held in place by a bobby pin — twice, as if afraid it will topple off and shame him. I like him doing that. It reminds me that he's not the enemy, but Jewish, like us. "A miracle cure," he goes on, fidgeting with his kipa once more. "Sulfa. You'll feel better in no time."

After a shaky start, when my fever spiked to 104 degrees and I felt like I was coughing up my lungs and the hospital cat would eat them for dinner, I agree with him. I'm breathing more easily, starting to improve.

The hospital is so overcrowded that the only bed available when I was admitted was next to that of a Polish yeshiva boy with pale translucent skin, perhaps from his illness, and a great shock of black hair that he's forever trying to smooth down and hide under his cap. When the boy's rabbi visited, he complained to our nurse about boys and girls being in the same room: "Forbidden." He glared at her.

"Nonsense," she said briskly, making my bed around me. "They're only children. Besides, there is nowhere else to put them. Would you prefer we let them die?"

The rabbi didn't answer, but his bristly eyebrows met in a frown as he pulled on his bushy beard. Eyes red-veined with anger, he turned and hobbled away.

The boy's name is Yoshi. He's very friendly, though he once whispered to me that he's not allowed to speak to females or have anything to do with them unless they're closely related to him. This taboo doesn't seem to deter him. "I'm a bad boy," he admits one day with a shark's grin. "I can always find a way around the rules."

Yoshi tells me his entire *yeshiva* escaped to Shanghai from Poland, leaving the students' families behind. They were worried about what Hitler might take it into his head to do to the religious Jews of Warsaw. We communicate quietly in Yiddish as he coils one of his corkscrew sidelocks around a finger. "What's wrong with you?" he asks.

"Pneumonia and sadness. Though the pneumonia part is almost better. They can't do anything about the sadness. You?"

"Don't know. They're trying to find out. *Stum*," he warns, when he hears someone coming. It's the nurse. She sits on Yoshi's bed and takes his temperature.

"Have a candy!" Yoshi leans over and produces one from behind her ear.

"Oh, Yoshi, you are a scream. I'll save it for my little girl."

She comes over to take my pulse. "I'm going to shut the window. The stink from the street below can't be good for your health," she says.

When she's gone, Yoshi continues our conversation in muffled tones, his cover drawn over his mouth as if he's a gangster, but his hands keep sneaking out and moving expressively as he speaks. "Talking to a girl in my community would be almost as bad as your making friends with a Nazi."

I suddenly can't breathe. Perhaps the pneumonia is returning. "As if I would," I protest, when I get my breath back. "The only Nazi I've ever had anything to do with was Hans, and he's my enemy, not my friend, although we were close before the Nazis took over. He joined the Hitler Youth. I've locked him away in my mind's vault, with *ACHTUNG* scrawled across its door in scarlet script, gory drops of blood dripping down to the floor."

Yoshi replies with a few words in a foreign language.

"What language is that?"

"English. The quote is by Shakespeare. He's my favourite. I can pick up any language just like that." He snaps his fingers.

"What's it mean?"

"'The lady doth protest too much, methinks.' Gertrude in *Hamlet*."

I don't understand what he's talking about, but am determined to learn English and read Shakespeare, in that order.

"Pick a card, any card," he says, taking a brilliantly coloured pack from beneath his covers and shuffling it expertly before fashioning it into a fan.

"Not now, I'm too tired." I turn my back on him and go to sleep.

CHAPTER 5

I continue to improve, and the nightmares are fading. One morning Mameh arrives to collect me, her face loaded with *maquillage*, her new sweater shimmering with diamantés. Over the neck of the sweater she's wearing a fake — at least, I imagine it's fake — emerald necklace. When she stands in the pool of light coming from the window, she glitters. She's visited every couple of days, perhaps sorry for treating me so badly while I was sick, though she'd rather die than admit it. I'm pleased to see her, as well as beyond grateful that she didn't have me sent back to Berlin. She's standing in front of me now, hands on hips, impatient. She glimmers in the half-light by my bed. "Hurry up and get dressed. I have an interview for a job this afternoon, must have a hairstyling and manicure before going. I can't take you with me. You look like a scarecrow."

"Thanks very much. You look like a Christmas tree."

"Enough of your lip, Freda. It's getting me down. I have to appear professional, childless. I can't be dragging you along with me everywhere. I need to get work and make some cash because I don't want to stay in that putrid *heim* for a moment longer than I ... *we* ... have to."

"*Heim?*" I ask. "What is a *heim*? A regular house like in Berlin?"

"No. A big building where they keep us new immigrants. Ugh. It's disgusting, like a prison. Uncleanable. One filthy blanket each; flies getting into everything; mice skittering around the floor; skeletal men leering at me; smelly children peeing and doing the other thing on the floor; ghastly food with insects in it at the *heim* kitchen."

"You don't have to work. You could sell the candlesticks." The silver candlesticks from home are the only objects of value we brought with us, the only heirlooms we still possess. Mameh wrapped them in my bedsheet and placed them in the bottom of our suitcase. I prayed the Nazis wouldn't find them when they searched us before we boarded the train. Thanks to Mameh's teasing them and batting her eyelashes, they were distracted enough to find nothing.

"Candlesticks, ha! They wouldn't get us very far. It's all very well for you." She sounds resentful. "You've been swaddled in blankets here, fed like a queen, and altogether treated like royalty."

"Huh? You think I got sick deliberately?"

"I wouldn't put it past you." She carries right on. "The *heim* is like something out of a horror film."

"I'll stay here then."

"Don't be an idiot. The hospital needs your bed. There are sick people lying on the floor in the hall. Though where you're going to sleep at the *heim* is another problem God has sent to vex me."

"Is New Oma still with us?"

"Yes. How could I let her go? She has to take care of Lotty, and now you as well, while I work." Her answer comforts me somewhat, though it demonstrates once again her selfishness. She *needs*, rather than *wants* New Oma to stay with us. At least, though, no matter what Mameh's motives are, there's someone to look after us in the frightful-sounding *heim*.

There's a sudden flurry of activity and the sound of people running up and down the hall. A nurse pokes her tortoise face into the room. "Hitler has invaded Poland, and Britain is at war with Germany," she announces with inappropriate glee. Withdrawing her head, she shuts the door.

"Is that good or bad?" I ask Mameh.

"Is what good or bad?"

"The war between the Nazis and the British."

She doesn't get a chance to answer.

"Depends on who you are," Yoshi murmurs, his mouth hidden beneath his blankets, as usual. "Maybe it'll take the Nazis' minds off the Jews. May God take care of all of us. I hope my family gets away. They sent me to the *yeshiva* when my mother heard that the school was leaving Poland."

"I hope they're safe. Fingers crossed," I murmur.

"Indeed. Thank you. I'll come and find you when I'm better. You can be my sister, at least till my own family turns up."

"You won't be allowed," says Mameh. "You, a *yeshiva* boy. Don't make me laugh. Your rabbi won't let you out."

"We'll see." He shoves his head defiantly above the blankets. "I can be the new Harry Houdini when it suits me. Freda, you know who Houdini was, don't you?"

"Yes. He was killed, I think, by someone punching him in the belly."

"He had appendicitis. Unlike him, I'll make sure to stay alive."

I hear a sob. I can just make out the downturned corners of his lips as he scrambles back under the covers. So he's not all happiness and conjuring tricks; despite his bravado, he's probably as frightened as I am.

I think of possible futures, feel as though I'm drowning.

CHAPTER 6

can't help but contrast the multiple clean avenues of Berlin — before Kristallnacht, that is — with the teeming streets of Hongkew near the hospital. As we walk toward the *heim*, I am shocked all over again at the stench and filth, the homeless children, the flea-ridden cats and dogs that don't seem to belong to anyone. Some of the buildings tower above us, modern and beautiful in design and execution. But narrow alleys contain homes jammed together like crooked teeth. There have been bombings in Shanghai, too many to count. I trip over rubble from shattered homes more than once, scraping my knees and the palms of my hands. Who lived here? Are they dead? I have no idea who bombed whom, but there can be no doubt that something appalling happened.

A Chinese baby like Becky — the doll I had as a small child, its face made of porcelain — lies in the mud. I bend over it, waving away a fly, wondering why anyone would leave such a helpless infant outside. Its open eyes are old and wise, as though it understands everything in the universe. But suddenly I realize that, like the man I saw on my way to the hospital, it's dead. It's been put out like garbage in a tiny woven basket.

"Don't touch it," says Mameh, "or you'll get sick all over again." She doesn't have to tell me. I've reeled back in fright and sorrow.

"Why did it die?"

"Disease, I expect. Or starvation. Something similar will happen to you if I don't get a job."

How can the Chinese die when there's so much to eat on the streets? Despite my disgust at the baby's death, my mouth fills with saliva at the tantalizing aroma of cooking food. Set out on tables and barrows are overflowing bowls of noodles and rice, as well as unidentifiable bits of vegetables and something that looks like fish. I guess these foodstuffs are for sale. I see copper coins pass between what appears to be a seller and an old man in a coolie hat. The man picks up a bowl of noodles and vegetables and uses chopsticks to push his meal into his mouth. I stare at him enviously, suddenly starving. "Let me have something, please," I beg Mameh.

"No, and don't you dare eat that food *ever*. The street vendors cook it in filthy river water."

Mameh really cares about me, after all. "Of course I won't eat it," I reply, "if you don't want me to."

"I certainly don't. I'm warning you, I won't look after you if you get sick from mucky street food. As it is you've had enough sickness to last a lifetime. There's not been two days in a row I haven't visited you while you've been in hospital, in case you died in the night. I've had to cope with running back and forth for weeks as well as working my fingers to the bone trying to clean our filthy corner of the *heim* because New Oma can't bend down any longer. I don't need anything else on my plate."

The bubble bursts. She's only thinking of herself, as usual. The first thing I'll do when she's out is run and fetch a bowl of noodles, even if I *do* get sick from them. It would be a small but satisfying rebellion. I'll have to figure out a way to make money to pay for the food and anything else that tempts me. Even a copper coin is beyond my means right now.

We are walking near enough to the water to hear the shouts of river folk. Their voices echo in my ears as the delicious cooking odour begins to blend with the rank smells of rotten fish, mouldy cabbage, and sewage. It's a nauseating mix. And I still have the pleasures of the *heim* awaiting me.

CHAPTER 7

For once Mameh isn't exaggerating. The *heim* is exactly as she described it. She, New Oma, and Lotty have been squashed into one corner of a large shabby room, its only furniture three small cots. The other refugees are in bunks, but perhaps whoever furnished the *heim* ran out of them before they reached our cubicle. We have less room than if we did have them — there's not any space between the cots — not to mention that with only three cots there's nowhere for me to sleep.

Lotty crawls to the end of her cot to greet me when I arrive. "I m-missed you, Freda," she cries, throwing her arms around me and squeezing. "I'm so g-glad you're here."

I hug her back. "I missed you too, Lotty." Strictly speaking this isn't true, but I've had time to do a lot of thinking in hospital, and I've again vowed not to be mean to her anymore. How long can my newfound kindness last? I haven't a clue. But Yoshi has lost all his family, at least for now, possibly forever. I should be grateful for what's left of mine.

I glance around. The paint is peeling and the plaster crumbling. There is a fine powdering of dust over everything, and spiders' webbed designs on the walls. Only my old bedsheet separates us from neighbouring families. It's slung over what appears to be a makeshift washing line, but there are still spaces at either end through which others can look. There must be at least twenty families in here, with no toilets or sinks, just what the woman in the next cubicle calls a honey bucket — a pail with a seat — and some basins. Lotty enthusiastically demonstrates what the honey buckets are for, but warns me not to sit on them, despite the seats, as New Oma says they'll spill. They have to be emptied every morning. I'm guessing that will be my job.

After a day I begin to sympathize with Mameh's desperation to leave. I can't get used to the noises and rank smells of people using the honey bucket right out in the open, as well as having to fight for a chance to brush my teeth and wash my face in the dirty water of the basin nearest us. I'm also covered in inflamed, terrifically itchy spots. Lotty has them too, and won't stop scratching.

"Oy yoy yoy. Bedbugs!" New Oma says when she sees our spots. She covers us with a cream she keeps in the pharmacy of her bag, afterwards rolling down our bedding and wiping disinfectant over the cots.

"C-come out, c-come out, wherever you are," yells Lotty, "you s-silly red bugs!"

"Shut up. They're not red bugs, they're bedbugs." I'm fed up with her. The bedbugs are nasty enough, but worse, the whole *heim* is overrun with other kinds of insects, particularly spiders, and spiders have always made me shudder. Platoons of them, unchecked, are on the move, crawling, scuttling, dangling from webs, watching, watching, watching. They are watching *me*. They are making sure I don't make a move to annihilate them. Not that I would. I'm too scared. There is also the occasional flying roach, and a scurrying under the beds that hopefully suggests mice rather than rats. I take care not to look in case they *are* rats. They carry terrible diseases, and I'd have to kill them. I hate to be the killer of anything.

"Remove it!" I remember screaming at Tateh when I saw a huge spider climbing up the wall in our Berlin house. "But don't kill it!"

"Then what do you expect me to do with it?"

"Uh, slide it onto a piece of card and leave it outside where I don't have to look at it."

"Sorry, but this one has met its fate. I'm not going to run after it with bits of paper." He knocked it onto the floor, stomped on it, and ground it into a black tangle of legs as though stubbing out one of his cigarettes.

"Hurray," Lotty cried, clapping her hands. Now, though, he's not here to squish even one soldier of the spiderly brigade. Perhaps he's been stomped on himself, in the camp the Nazis have no doubt sent him to. The thought is so horrible I gag.

CHAPTER 8

Since there are only three cots, Mameh and I share one. They are so narrow I can barely breathe, and every time I move, even to rub my nose or scratch a bite, Mameh angrily hisses at me to stop fidgeting. I finish the night in Lotty's bed. But eventually, after clip-clopping daily on her high heels around Hongkew, Mameh obtains an evening job, or "my employment" as she calls it in a mincing way. She applies her *maquillage* each evening before she goes out, reflecting herself in a large broken mirror she found on the street and hung on our wall.

She's incredibly secretive about her work. Her only reply was, "It doesn't matter," when I asked what she did, and her expression deterred my asking more questions. I caught the lady in the next cubicle rolling her eyes at Mameh's answer. Why would that be?

But I don't really care what she does as it means I have the cot to myself every night and can scratch any part of me I want to. I can at last sleep on my tummy — my favourite position — breathing in stale traces of her scent and cigarette smoke. In my mind I call it "the Mameh smell." I have to vacate the cot for her early in the morning. If I oversleep, she turfs me out so she, exhausted, can climb in. "Go *do* something, for heaven's sake," she snarls. But apart from lining up outside the *heim* kitchen to eat the usual bland and sparse meals three times a day, and asking people if there are any little jobs they'd like done — there aren't, as they're too hard up to pay me — there's nothing much to keep me busy except watching her snore, searching out where the spiders and bedbugs have got to, and shushing Lotty.

I wander away from the *heim* whenever I can, but this week the weather has been wintry. Nonetheless, one day I feel that if I'm cooped up in our miserable corner any longer, I'll scream the place down, so I tiptoe out of the room and down the stairs of the building in search of what I promised myself ages ago — noodles. They'll warm my belly. It's ice-cold outside. Winter is closing in. The sky has a green cast to it and a clap of thunder sounds nearby, echoing along the alleyways. A few wet snow-flakes flutter down, and I catch them on my tongue.

I'm so glad I brought my coat from Berlin, though it's even tighter under the arms now. I'm still wearing my old boots, though I've repeatedly asked Mameh to buy me new ones. After tottering along the road, my toes feeling as if they're in a vise, I spy several stalls arrayed with bowls of noodles and rice. I can almost taste them. Saliva floods my mouth. One of the vendors has her back turned, so I creep over to steal a handful of noodles, which I imagine taste like ambrosia. I barely get a noodle into my mouth before the woman wheels around and sees me. "Hei, hei, hei," she shrieks.

Suddenly, passersby are glaring at me. I take off down the street, but the boots kill, and like a lame dog, I start to limp. The vendor catches up to me, grabs one of my braids, and pulls till it feels like a thousand needles are stabbing my scalp. She slaps my hands so hard that the noodles cascade onto the ground. At the same time she lets fly a torrent of singsong words, none of which I understand.

An old man translates: "Lady say if you catched stealing again, she call police. Hongkew police big men. Put you in jail." He wags his finger at me.

Shamed at being caught, feeling the blood rise in my cheeks, I slink back to the *heim*. For weeks I'm afraid to wander out again. Because I'm so bored with being penned in, I become disobedient and raucous. I hang around making a general nuisance of myself and fighting with my sister, despite my earlier good intentions. I want to make her suffer what I've suffered, even if that means pulling *her* hair till she screams. Others in the *heim* complain. New Oma, perplexed, doesn't know what to make of my loud-mouthed and disruptive behaviour, and Mameh can't sleep for the din I'm making. When she slaps me, I yell even louder. It's a mystery to me. I want to stop but can't. When she hears word of a new free school starting nearby, Mameh enrolls me. Both of us breathe a sigh of relief.

In December 1939, as war begins to rage in Europe, and Mameh lights candles in her two silver candlesticks because it's Chanukah, I become a student at the school for Jewish children on Kinchow Road.

1940

The Year of the Dragon

CHAPTER 9

On the first day, New Oma and Lotty accompany me so I don't get lost. How could I? It's only a few steps from the *heim*, and I'm more sure of the way than New Oma is, as I've searched out its location by following schoolgirls and -boys to their destination over the past few days. But today I'm nervous. It's been years since I've attended school. The Nazis passed harsh laws regarding the Jews. One of them was to close the doors of schools against all Jewish children. We were locked out. Will I be able to keep up? Will the other students like me, not spit at me the way children did in Germany? I'm glad to have Lotty and New Oma for support.

"I w-want to go to school too," Lotty cries.

"School isn't for babies," I retort. Feeling a throb of remorse, I add, "You'll be able to come soon, when you're five. Won't be long now."

She nods happily, then skips back down the road. New Oma, bent-backed, follows her slowly, after taking me around to wish me luck. I feel lonely, deserted, as they disappear. There is nothing for it but to follow the other students into the building. They don't spit at me or whisper to one another like the students used to in Berlin. They simply turn and stare at me curiously. One girl, who stands alone, speaks to me in Yiddish. "Don't I know you from the Ward Street *heim?*"

"Yes," I say, happy to have someone to speak to.

"That's where I live too, for my sins."

"I'm Freda."

"My name's Gertrude, or Gert as my mameh calls me, but either way I hate the name. Gert sounds to me like a tight corset. Gertrude, ugh, sounds like someone with sweaty boots."

Sweaty boots? She really does have a talent for odd sayings. "Gertrude is a character in *Hamlet,*" I say, hoping I sound both serious and knowledgeable. I've been reading Shakespeare furtively in German at a bookshop, when I've not been banging around making a nuisance of myself. A hoyden, Mameh calls me.

Gertrude looks at me blankly before continuing. "There are too many sweaty boots in the *heim* already, smelling like mouldy sheep, hanging from hooks — the boots that is, not the sheep — or left at the ends of beds as if waiting for St. Nicholas to fill them with chocolate and candies at Christmas."

"What a thing for a Jewish girl to say!" I begin to laugh.

"Stop cackling, if you please. I'm sure if we had chandeliers the offending articles would be dangling by their laces from them, too."

"Doubtless." I try to hide my mirth, but it bubbles out of my throat till I wheeze and my lungs begin to hurt.

"Perhaps you don't understand my agony over being called such an atrocious name because your name's Freda. Freda's a regular, everyday sort of name, not at all like Gertrude. My brother Dedrick once told me that the name Gertrude sounded like overcooked beetroot. I told him his name sounded like a dead rat. I'm sorry I said that now because the Nazis took him away with my father. I may never see him again." She makes a harsh noise, half sob and half snort. "Even so, where did my parents dig up such names?" She knits her heavy eyebrows in consternation.

I'm attempting to say something, but all I can manage is a gasp of laughter. Gertrude races on like a horse cantering down a steep hill. "Just a minute, just a minute, if you please, Freda, and then you can have your say. Isobella suits me much better. It sounds like fairy bells tinkling. Or Izo for short, though it sounds like soap powder. You can call me that. I won't be offended." She grins and two dimples appear, one on each side of her mouth. The grin disappears. Her expression becomes earnest; her eyes are a piercing green. I've forgotten what I meant to say, have no idea why she thinks Gertrude sounds like stinky boots, or Izo sounds like a make-believe soap powder, or for that matter why fairy bells suit a girl who is at least twice as wide as I am. But none of it matters. Someone in school is speaking to me!

"I just know we're going to be friends," she says. I agree, already love her for her off-kilter wit. I feel enormously pleased at her words, am thrilled to be accepted as she introduces me to some of the other girls and leads me to class.

1941

The Year of the Snake

CHAPTER 10

adore school. It's what I've wanted since being forbidden to go to classes in Berlin. Instruction is in English, which I pick up very fast. I love the sound of it: it's gentler and softer than either German or Yiddish, neither of which is spoken in class. Mr. Kadoorie, the benefactor of the school, doesn't like the German language, I suppose because it reminds him of the Nazis. The teacher says I'm a quick study, and I beam. I quickly become the top student in my class, and the headmistress says I'm going to be a great success. At what, I'm not quite sure. The future is like a rainbow, bright with possibility.

"A writer? A clockmaker like Tateh?" I ask New Oma. "Or should I go to university after the war is over? Perhaps become a doctor." My thoughts are as muddled as the twists and turns of the Whangpoo River.

"Don't fret your head, *maidel*. You'll know when you know."

I only hope she's right. I'm overwhelmed by indecision.

Izo and I have become firm friends and allies. But I have to watch her hands. She's an inveterate shoplifter, "a snapper-up of unconsidered trifles" — I'm working hard at Shakespeare — and her sticky fingers could get us both into trouble. I remonstrate with her when after a visit to the market she opens her hand to reveal a pair of earrings. "It's fun," she replies.

"Not for me." I still burn with embarrassment because I tried to swipe noodles from a Chinese vendor and was almost arrested. I've not stolen so much as a rubber band since. It would take something of life-or-death importance for me to ever steal anything — especially food — again, and at the moment I don't need to. The school provides us with milk and free lunches to build our muscles and help us grow tall. When Izo steals I turn the other way, pretend we're not together. I've even wondered once or twice whether I should report her to our teacher, but know in my heart it's something I would never do, because if I did I could never forgive myself.

The wealthier students, whose families can afford apartments, as well as private lessons in music or tennis or ballet for their children, look down their noses at us as if there's a bad smell in the room. They also refer to us as *"heim* rats." I pretend not to care, as in the afternoons, when they are whisked away to their various activities, we *heim* rats take gym, and afterwards play ball games outside.

Even though I hate the rich students at least twice as much as they hate me, I don't show it, hoping against hope that one day one of them will invite me to a birthday or Chanukah party at her home. No one ever does, though. I long to be like them, to have piano or dance lessons and money of my own. It took me forever to badger Mameh into buying me boots that fit, and now, shooting up like a weed, I'm outgrowing the new ones. I want a puppy, but I can't have one in the *heim*; we wouldn't be able to pay for its food, anyhow. I long for us to find somewhere to live that's cleaner and more agreeable.

I begin to feel desperate. I hate the constant coming and

going of the other refugees, the smoking, the snoring concertos at night, the stale sweaty stink of so many people contriving to live in such a small space without proper washing facilities. I stink too. The wealthy students aren't wrong on that score. I need a bath so I can wash my hair properly and get the horrid smell that clings to me to go away, but a hot bath costs a penny, so I can't have more than one a month. The rest of the time I have to sluice down in a basin. When I begin to have periods, the need for both washing and privacy becomes even more dire.

"Use a rag under your knickers and stop whining," says Mameh, whose eyes are as usual clotted with mascara after she returns from work.

I long for better meals too, especially on the weekends when I'm not in school. The amount of food we get at the *heim* is dwindling, and has gone from three meals a day to two, and recently to one. I'm luckier than Lotty, though, because I get that free lunch during the week. Sometimes I manage to bring her home a piece of bread or meat or cheese, but she's no longer roly-poly. I'm afraid if she's not fed more she'll end up like the dead Chinese babies in the alleyways of Hongkew. Every afternoon, to take her mind off her constant hunger, I try to teach her some of what I've learned. New Oma, who must also be hungry, watches us with one eye, her other eye shut, lost in the multiple creases of her face. She worries primarily about our welfare. Under her care, Lotty has gained confidence and has all but lost her stammer. She will be able to go to kindergarten in the new year and receive lunches.

Mameh continues to stow money under the mattress she shares with me, using it only to buy new dresses or lipstick and scent for work. She must have a fortune hidden under the bed in candlesticks and cash; she doesn't put much store in banks ever since a bank in Berlin confiscated our savings. As I grow older I begin to wonder what she does at night when she vanishes like a perfumed spectre from the *heim*, sometimes staying away for a day or even longer, making me nervous that she won't come back; but she stays *stum* on the subject.

"If you were a boy you'd have had your bar mitzvah in September. You'd be considered a man. So you're not a little girl any longer. You're a woman. I want you to quit school and come to work with me," she says one evening, as she's dolling herself up for her mysterious "employment."

"Nothing doing." I see my reflection as well as hers in the shard of silvered glass that she calls her mirror. I look annoyed if not downright angry. My eyes are black as midnight and my lips turned down in a grimace, so I quickly tack around and stare out of the window. It's just the two of us, Mameh and me, standing behind the threadbare sheet that partially shields us from the prying eyes of others in the *heim*. New Oma and Lotty have gone for a walk in a park close by.

"It would be a great help financially, and my boss is looking for fresh girls." Mameh's tone has softened. She is attempting to cajole me into obedience.

Fresh girls strikes me as a particularly odious term. What has her boss done with the stale ones?

"Not interested." I keep my back to her.

"We could do with the extra cash. It'll get us out of the *heim* faster."

"I told you I'm not interested. I hate makeup and fussy gowns and high heels. I hate dressing up the way you do. I hate the thought of leaving school. I want to make something of myself after the war is over. Besides, we could get out of the *heim* without my help. You must have more than enough money tucked under the mattress to rent an apartment. I've no idea why we're still here."

"Landlords charge more cash than I can put away. By the time I've finished looking after the four of us and making myself presentable to go to work, I don't have a *Pfennig*. See?" She shakes out her jacket and inside-outs the pockets, as Lotty would say. I don't believe Mameh. Not for one minute. She pleaded poverty to the Jewish Relief Committee so pays nothing for our spot at the *heim* and next to nothing for anything else. She was even able to take out a small loan, which soon vanished. Money slides through her fingers like water; I don't know what she spends it on besides what she wears for what she coyly calls her "employment." What I do know, though, is that none of it was spent on us, my boots being the only exception, so I wouldn't catch pneumonia again.

New Oma once asked for the wherewithal to feed us, but Mameh said she couldn't afford to give anything, and wasn't there plenty of food in the *heim* kitchen? I waited for New Oma to argue with her, but she bit her tongue, which is probably the right approach to take with Mameh. "With your mother," she always says, "it's best not to fight." But I can't seem to stop myself.

"You don't look after us. You disappear for days, so we are left to look after one another. And you don't spend your earnings on us. You spend them on making yourself more glamorous, and God knows what else. Lotty is close to starving. New Oma goes hungry so she can feed her — and me on the weekends."

"I can't deal with this. Next time I leave, it'll be for good."

Mameh's suggestions, or rather demands, can be outrageous, especially where money's concerned. So New Oma's made a habit of taking Lotty and me to the market when she can. She can't afford to buy on the second floor, where the vendors are mostly European, selling sausages, herring, meat, and cheese. On the first floor the sellers are Chinese, and the food is cheap, plentiful, and filling. She lets us pick out whatever we want and pays for it out of her purse, which must be almost drained. What will we do when the tap runs dry?

"You have to earn a living, Freda," Mameh continues, "or we'll never be able to move away from here."

"I don't want to work with you, and that's flat. Your generation got an education, didn't they, if they wanted one?"

"Different times." She shrugs her shoulders. "In any case, I hated school and was glad to leave."

"We're talking about me, not you. I *love* school, and the headmistress says I'll earn my international certificate if I keep on."

"Oh, hoity-toity. Princess Snotty and Smug of Shanghai. Too good for the rest of us, are you? No wonder you keep getting too big for your boots."

"Is that an attempt to be funny?" I ask, trying to stay calm. "Listen, Mameh, I need to stay in school. I'm nowhere near old enough to go out to work. I don't know what you do, and I'm not sure I want to know. There's an immoral smell to it."

"There's no use my having morals in Shanghai, because nobody else does."

"Then for certain I don't want to do it." I often imagine possibilities. Perhaps she's having a good time with men now that Tateh's missing, and is being paid for her favours.

"I want you to come and work where I work, at the Green Lily Café. It's a respectable establishment. Extras," she simpers, "are voluntary. Up to you whether you take advantage of them or not. I greet the café's customers; I show them to their seats and hand out menus; and I smile, smile, smile till the skin of my cheeks cracks and my teeth grind together. I dance with men for tickets they buy that I can change back to cash. That's what being a hostess is all about, as if you didn't know. And to be honest, I'm sick of it. I only do it for the sake of the family."

"What you're describing is disgraceful. And I'm sure I haven't heard the half of it. Yet you want me to quit school and do it too?"

"I need you to share the load."

"No, Mameh! I'm already doing as much as I can. How can you even suggest it? I'm having lessons at the headmistress's house while school is closed and we wait to move to a new building. She's only tutoring her brightest and most hard-working students. And besides, what you're describing sounds like prostitution. It's probably the reason that you don't come back to the *heim* some mornings. Ugh! How could you do what you do? You're a married woman."

"A widow, more like. I'll *make* you leave. We can't afford for you to keep on at school."

"We?"

"I." She blushes.

I'm furious. "Rubbish. It costs you nothing. Tateh would shout at you to let me stay on. He values a good education, was heartbroken when I was excluded from school in Berlin. Taught me himself whenever he could. He would be incensed at your scandalous behaviour, not to mention your trying to push me into becoming scandalous myself."

Mameh doesn't respond, merely shakes her head. The thought of Tateh seems to have defeated her. She sits at the end of the bed, hunched like an old, old woman, even older than New Oma. Her mascara is beginning to melt, coating her cheeks with tarry black lines that run outwards from her eyes like spiders' legs. Her own legs are swinging backward and forward, reminding me of someone I saw on the street once who was having a seizure. In our shadowed corner, as dusk begins to paint our one window a dark, starless grey, she appears macabre, witchy.

I've won our battle, at least for the present, by invoking Tateh's name and his almost certain anger at what she's doing to herself and trying to do to me. My triumph makes me cruel. "Don't go to work till you fix your face. You look like a whore. I'm ashamed of you," I retort, knocking the last nail into the coffin before banging out the door for an *Oneg Shabbat*. I'm sure of myself, strong, righteous. As I swagger from the *heim*, I recall my old friend Hans, his dark birthmark, his honey-hued eyes. The image of him and his Hitler Youth friends swaggering their way down the street floods my brain, leaving me contrite and desperately mortified.

Mameh wasn't always like this. When I was a small child she ran her fingers through my hair lovingly. She kissed and cuddled me and helped me cut pictures of models out of her fashion magazines so I could make plays with them. Then we acted them out together. But by the time Lotty came along, Mameh had changed. She totally abandoned her to Tateh's care. I blamed it on her fear of what would happen in the future as our lives grew bleaker. But in truth, I can't blame the Nazis for everything.

"Don't ever speak to your mother like that again." It's Tateh, scolding me for berating her while using his name to do so. Dead or alive, he speaks via a secret conduit into my mind. I will need to apologize to Mameh in the morning.

But I don't get a chance. When I awake I hear a low buzz that encircles the *heim*. As more refugees realize the import of what's happening, they begin to cry and shriek, their voices rising in a dreadful crescendo. The noise, growing ever more piercing, wakens Lotty and New Oma. We huddle together, feeling that it's the end of the world, at least for us.

A great bear of a refugee climbs on the table and yells above the din: "*Stum*, everybody, I have breaking news. For those who haven't yet heard: The Japanese have bombed Pearl Harbor in Hawaii, sinking most of the U.S. ships that are lying in port and revealing their true colours. Now they are the official allies of the Nazis, enemies of *our* allies."

I shudder. The Americans will have to join the war now. They have no choice. We will wait in fear for our lives to change, for the war to expand even more, for the Nazis to grow stronger with the assistance of the Japanese. For the moment, all remains as usual, at least for us.

But early the next day the Japanese take over Shanghai, and soon after Germany declares war on America.

That evening we hear heavy bombardment coming from the area of Shanghai's harbour. Lotty is terrified. The sky lights up, brilliant with a military fireworks display. The roar of guns rocks Hongkew. Lotty is now screaming with her hands clapped over her ears, as I attempt to pacify her. Others are shouting, pacing, sobbing. Our one window has been shattered by the blasts, our cots covered in glass. It feels like Kristallnacht revisited. New Oma, unaware of anything that's happening, is sleeping through the constant blasts of artillery. Perhaps she's going deaf. I take Lotty into bed with me after shaking my blanket free of glass, and we huddle together beneath it for the rest of the night. I can still hear explosions and see gigantic flashes through our threadbare cover, until morning springs open like a jack-in-the-box and the fusillade ceases.

I hear Lotty saying, "That was the worst thunderstorm ever," before I fall into a deep, dreamless sleep. In the afternoon, I gather from a refugee, who has trekked down to the harbour to see what's happening, that apparently the Japanese navy has sunk a British gunboat after taking over another. The war has reached its long arm across the Pacific to shatter the uneasy peace of Shanghai.

1942

The Year of the Horse

CHAPTER 11

One evening, a hand snakes into our cubicle and knocks on the wall, followed by its owner, a tall woman from one of the Jewish Agencies, whom I've seen before, but wished never to see again.

"I'm looking for a Malka Isen. I've been told she lives here," she says in a high, no-nonsense voice.

"Malka Isen is my m-mother," I stammer, sounding like Lotty. "She's at work right now, but I can give a message to her when she returns." I am quaking from my head to my fingertips. This is the woman who's all too often the bringer of bad news, telling the refugees that one or another person in their family has died, usually in the camps. Around here she's known as the angel of death. I steel myself against disaster. I'm already grieving.

Her voice softens. "No need to be afraid, little lady," she says, drawing a tattered envelope from her bag. "It's not a message of the dead or missing I'm bringing. This letter's been all over the place, almost around the world, you might say. It took the agency a while to find you people, but I was so sure you'd want a letter from a dear one that I searched till I tracked you down."

I take a deep breath before thanking her profusely. After she leaves, I examine the envelope, my fingers still trembling. It's from Tateh! He always had a bold hand, easy to identify. The address reads, "To Frau Malka Isen and Family, via the Jewish Agency." I can't breathe, I'm so excited. Should I open the letter myself or wait for Mameh? The address does read *and Family*, but I ask New Oma's advice.

"Open it, open it, Freda. I'm sure your mother won't object." I'm not as certain as New Oma is, but I'm going to open it anyway. I can't wait hours for Mameh to return, if she returns at all. I try to hold back my tears as I read what's inside to New Oma and Lotty:

My dearest Malka, Freda, and Annalotte,

As you probably know, I've been taken to a labour camp. The commandant has said that prisoners with a place to go to outside Germany may be released soon. I thought of my cousin Ben in Canada. One of the staff says he'll smuggle this letter out. You are on my mind every minute of every day, and I can't wait to see you. I miss you all so much, but please God this will find you and we may soon be a family again.

All my love, Shmuel (Tateh)

"Tateh's coming, Tateh's coming," screams Lotty, hugging herself with glee.

"Wonderful," says New Oma. "Something to hope for."

When Mameh comes back from work, I hand her the letter, and Lotty tells her the good news in a loud screech that encourages a man in another cubicle to yell at her to shut up or he'll come over and clock her one.

"Idiots," Mameh hisses at us. "Why didn't you bother to look at the date? This was written almost two years ago."

CHAPTER 12

This evening, I've promised to meet Izo and Yoshi as usual at the *Oneg Shabbat* in the Ward Street synagogue after the Friday night service. We'll be able to share cake, cookies, apples, and pears, my only supper. Yoshi will be in disguise, with his sidelocks pushed behind his ears, his *kipa* in a pocket, and his long fringed *tsitsis* tucked under his shirt. He wears a scarf that's so short it barely covers his bony neck, and he waves his hands in the air like a conjurer; he usually dresses and acts this way when he escapes from the *yeshiva*. I half expect him to magick up a rabbit or a dove.

The first time I saw him in his odd getup I didn't recognize him, though his skin was still the colour of washed linen, his body slender and frail as a willow branch, and his black hair sticking up in all directions. It looked as if he'd stuck his finger in an electric socket. "It's me, Freda, Yoshi!" he shouted.

Other students, more obedient than we are, arrived earlier to pray, so deserve the treats. We probably don't. Izo and I skipped the service and have returned to catch up with Yoshi, to eat, and to discuss what he calls a grave matter. A few threads of his *tsitsis* escape from under his shirt and float in the evening air as he comes to greet Izo and me. We have vital ideas to discuss, but food comes before anything else. We rush to reach it before it disappears. Yoshi is at the table first.

In a trice he's cramming chocolate cake and jam cookies into his mouth. He even finds some ragged crusts of *chaleh* left over from the service and devours them too. He's always starving. Though the *yeshiva* meals are much better than ours at the *heim* and in school, Yoshi never puts on an ounce. In fact, he looks as though he's lost a few pounds since I last saw him, and it worries me. But he's unwilling to talk about his thinness or pallor, and puts his hand over my mouth when I try to discuss it with him. Could he have a tapeworm? Surely the doctor would have discovered it when he was in the hospital. But the doctor told Yoshi to go back to the *yeshiva* because he couldn't find anything wrong with him.

Despite his sickness — if indeed it is a sickness — and the doctor's failure to diagnose it, Yoshi remains high-spirited. He's also the kindest and most generous person I know, who thinks of others before he considers himself. Sometimes he makes a supreme sacrifice by bringing around *yeshiva* leftovers for Lotty instead of eating them himself. She loves him for it. I'm beginning to love him too, at least in a sisterly way. But I'm worried about Izo, who stares at him soulfully, with eyes that seem both hopeful and desperate.

Mameh woke up one morning when Yoshi was bringing food to my sister. Shouting so loudly that others turned to see who was making such a racket, she tossed him out of our spider-web of a corner. "If you come back I'll inform your rabbi," she stormed, angry at having her sleep disturbed, "and then won't you be in for it?" He vanished in less than a second, a pocketful of silver cutout stars he'd no doubt brought for

Lotty drifting to the floor in his wake; but Mameh's anger didn't deter him. He still flits in while she's sleeping, his prayer shawl tassels often coming free and floating out behind him. His wizard hands flash before our eyes, uncovering a treat for Lotty or a flower for me.

Ours is a give-and-take relationship. Yoshi brings gifts for us and favours us with his presence; Lotty, New Oma, and I supply a ready-made family for him, as his own is still missing. He often spirits us outside to avoid waking Mameh, though people stare at his strange costume. He tells New Oma to pick a card. He produces a gold foil coin full of bubblegum from behind Lotty's ear. His magical presence washes my mind free of the *heim*. Yesterday he brought me a rose. Today, for the *Oneg*, he brings his will-o'-the-wispy self.

After every scrap of food is finished and all of us have sung Hebrew songs and exuberantly danced so fast that the girls' feet leave the floor in a flying hora, the room grows quiet and empty, leaving behind only the three of us and two women who are stacking dirty dishes. We settle against a back wall and speak in whispers. Or at least Yoshi and I do. We have to remind Izo to turn down the volume.

"You act like I'm a radio," she counters, too loudly.

"Shh, this is serious," I whisper. "We're forming a secret society. Yoshi already told me about it, after he discussed it with the Jewish Underground."

"We are about to form the Junior Jewish Resistance in Shanghai. The JJRS." Yoshi's voice is low and sounds official; but his fingers, ungovernable, rise from his lap to weave patterns in the air.

"So you say. What I'm itching to understand is who we're supposed to be resisting."

"The Japanese," says Yoshi.

"The Nazis," I assert. Neither Yoshi nor I really know. We haven't untangled the threads yet. Shanghai is a very complicated city, with three main areas — the French Concession, the International Settlement, and Hongkew, which is really part of the Settlement too. It's incredibly confusing. The Japanese and Chinese had an air fight in 1937, just before the refugees started to arrive, and between them bombed many buildings in Shanghai. The Japanese are very visible now in Hongkew, which consists mainly of Chinese nationals, Jewish immigrants, and some of the worse-off Japanese themselves. It's the poorest area of Shanghai, a den of thieves, as some of my wealthier schoolmates call it with a nasty twist of the lips. But there's a rumour that the Japanese army is conquering the whole of China city by city as they travel south toward Shanghai. I wait, almost impatiently, for their tanks and planes, their platoons of troops, their foot soldiers to arrive. Let's get it over with. Let's see what horrible fate they have in store for us. Better to know than spend my time wondering and fearful.

I have an idea. "The Japanese are already in charge, in the cafés, in the streets, in the International Settlement. They are paving the way for an onslaught. We can take advantage of them before the tanks arrive, steal food rations from the fraction of the Japanese Army that's already here, and distribute them to the starving." It sounds so easy, as if we're do-or-dare characters in a children's adventure story.

I remember thinking that it would take something of life-or-death importance for me to ever steal anything again. This is definitely life-or-death important. We could save all the starving Chinese babies so they wouldn't end up in little woven baskets on the streets waiting to be taken to the trash. And at the same time we can hurt the Japanese Machine as its tanks plough through the country, likely killing and plundering. "If we can appropriate enough food, they will have to do their plundering on empty stomachs, at least in Shanghai."

"That's inspired, Freda. How do you propose we do it?" asks Yoshi.

"I don't know, but I do know that Izo has sticky fingers, and you, Yoshi, have the quickest, wickedest fingers in the world. We'll manage it without a problem. We'll strategize and come up with a plan. Then we'll hold practice drills."

Just then the two cleanup women push us out of the synagogue and into the chilly night, locking the door behind us.

"Sounds exciting." Yoshi gives me a friendly pat on the back by way of congratulation. Izo is staring at Yoshi with cow eyes as though he's forgotten she's there. She doesn't spare a look for me. Yoshi notices her rapt stare too. "Here you go, Miss Sticky Fingers," he says, beaming. Conjuring a brightly wrapped Chinese candy out of the air, he gives it to Izo with a flourish. "Enjoy. It's the last one I have. For the time being, anyway."

"Don't worry. I can easily get you more. The market is full of them," boasts Izo, happy once more, dropping the candy onto her stuck-out tongue and drawing it slowly into her mouth. I watch as she sucks the soft centre out of it. I watch as she chews. I watch as she swallows. "I too can steal food rations, and even a bit of *matériel* if necessary," she says.

"That's terrific, Izo," applauds Yoshi, kissing her on the cheek. "I knew we could count on you. We'll call what we're involved in the first military action of the JJRS, or even better, Operation Sticky Fingers. The Underground has said it has a few simple, though possibly dangerous, jobs for us, delivering messages, that kind of thing. Remember, not a word to anyone!" As he speaks, his luminous eyes fixed on Izo's, my cheeks grow hot, my hands sweaty. A sharp stab of jealousy punctures my heart. It bleeds profusely as Izo begins to laugh.

1943

The Year of the Sheep

CHAPTER 13

School has resumed in the new building on East Yuhang Road. I'm thrilled to be back in the classroom, and work hard every evening to keep my grades up. But I can barely sleep, lie awake until three or four in the morning tossing one way and then the other, terrified at having heard a rumour that the Nazis and Japanese have discussed exterminating all the Jews in Shanghai. Thank God it hasn't happened yet. I'm sleepless for so long that I see the cinnamon dawn travel like an incoming tide across our window, splashing us with the sun's first rays. I rise tired-eyed to go to school. I fumble with my buttons. I forget to remember my notebook and arrive without pencils. Izo is at the entrance, so I start worrying about her and Yoshi.

I can't stop myself condemning them for their treacherous relationship. I keep replaying what happened between them as my marks plummet. At least their obvious love distracts me somewhat from thoughts about my own demise.

I absolutely hate Izo, despise her, loathe and detest her, although I still pretend in school that she's my best friend. She's an ass. Her loud braying tortures my brain; her hair looks like the wood shavings in my old rabbit hutch in Berlin. Besides her ugly red face and witchy eyes, she's a nasty, greedy thief. I wonder why I never noticed how horrid she was before. Wrapped in my cocoon of misery and anger, I've all but forgotten that her bold thievery is the foundation of our present enterprise.

But Yoshi? How can he be in love with her? How can he adore her murky green eyes and not my velvety brown ones? How can he prefer her haystack curls to my long chestnut braids? It's a mystery. I thought he cared for me, but all along it was Izo he was interested in. He used me to get to her. Ugh. Disgraceful. And now that he has what he wants he doesn't even visit. He came once or twice after our last *Oneg* meeting to give me messages from the Underground to hide in my bag and deliver on my way to or from school, but I've heard nothing from him since, not even to ask me how my deliveries went. I need to tell him that some people were too frightened to open their doors, so I still possess some of the messages, which could be dangerous for me and, I suppose, for them. I burn with resentment of him and envy of Izo, even though I never felt anything but friendship for him before what I think of as "The Incident."

After a long, mysterious absence, he turns up at the *heim* late one night. He ducks under our privacy sheet with a pear for Lotty — who is growing round again from school lunches — and a sprig of jasmine for me.

Some neighbours are playing cards by candlelight in the next cubicle. I'd been lying awake, listening to them make bids, when Yoshi arrived. It's a moonlit night so I can see him plainly. Mameh is on the lam again for the second day — not that she'd be home now, as she's supposed to be at her "employment" — and Lotty and New Oma are asleep. The pear smells ripe and sweet but is soon overwhelmed by the rich perfume of the jasmine, which fills our cubicle. Yoshi drops the pear on Lotty's pillow next to her decrepit Mimi doll, which she brought from Berlin. I reject the jasmine and turn my back on him, red spots of rage dancing in front of my eyes.

He sits on the edge of my cot. The springs squeak, and he bounces once or twice more to make an even louder noise. When I continue to face the wall, he whistles to get my attention. "Ladies and gentlemen," he announces, "a concerto for mattress, tin whistle, and bed springs!" He pauses. "What's the matter, Freda? I came to see you specially. I haven't been before because I was caught escaping from the *yeshiva* and locked up at bedtime for a month. I told the rabbi I was going down to the Whangpoo River to sail an origami boat, but for some reason he didn't believe me, maybe because I had no origami."

"How sad," I say sarcastically. "Stop bouncing around. You're bumping me. Have you been seeing Izo?"

"Don't be silly. Why would I?"

I face him. "Because you kissed her cheek and glanced at her meaningfully."

"Like this?" He makes a gorilla face, goggling his eyes, and though I want to stay stern and disapproving, I can't help but smile.

"No. More as if you're dying for love of her."

"I have no idea what you're talking about. But if I did do something of the sort, it was because she was looking left out and lonely, as she usually does when we're all together. It meant nothing to me."

"So you're not in love with her?"

"In love with Izo?" He groans. Both his voice and his hands rise, his fingers fluttering in a language of their own. "I should say not. She's *your* friend to the end, not mine."

"Shh," I say. "You'll wake Lotty and New Oma."

"I'm not *in* love with anyone. But I do love you. You're my replacement sister, Castor to my Pollux, my best pal in the world … in sickness and in health, as the Gentiles say."

I'm so touched by his words that they bring me to tears, but to hide them I ask, sniffing, who Castor and Pollux are.

"They were mythical twin boys," he replies. "You should read more."

"And were you really locked up?"

"Of course. The rabbi was trying to save my soul by turning the key, though I fear it's too late. There's no use locking the gate after the *yeshiva* boy has escaped. I've had a taste of the world and need to return to it. Why would I lie?"

"No reason." I grin as I accept the jasmine the second time it's offered, and, sitting, pull his arm around me, as I used to do with Tateh. We hug for a moment before he jumps off the bed, kissing my hand with an exaggerated flourish.

"I must go. I can't risk getting into more trouble. One of the older boys prowls around at midnight to make sure we're all in our beds."

I give him the undelivered messages, with a short explanation of why I still have them. "Good night, brother Pollux," I whisper as he leaves. I imagine him climbing through a window at the *yeshiva*; tiptoeing across the floor to his bed; restraining the shadow play of his eloquent fingers; and all in all doing his best to avoid detection. He must have picked the jasmine from a bush in someone's yard, and swiped the pear from the market. Either that, or he magicked them both up.

CHAPTER 14

I wake with a start. Someone is yelling in my ear. Perhaps the *heim* is on fire. Which well it might be, given all the whisperings that the war between the Japanese and Chinese is heating up again. I expect a bomb to drop on us every day. But it's only Lotty. "Go away," I cry. "I'm trying to sleep."

"Get up, get up right now. We're going to be late for school."

How can that be? Though still half in and half out of a dream, I realize something must be wrong. Again. Mameh usually elbows me out of our bed so she can slide into it. Then I wake the others so they don't oversleep. But today, according to both New Oma and Lotty, she's nowhere to be found.

"I w-went and looked up and down the road, but I couldn't see her," grumbles Lotty.

"You know your mother, *shaina maidel*. She's maybe having ... an early breakfast with friends ... or a shower in the bathhouse. She's been gone before, and always comes back. Might be looking ... at rooms to rent ... so we can get out of the *heim*, yes?"

"No," I reply, as I struggle into my blouse, which is far too small and pinches me under the arms. The buttons keep popping open. "That'll be the day."

"Don't worry your head about it now. Take Lotty's hand ... and go to class before you get ... a black mark." New Oma's voice is much more raspy and her breathing even noisier than usual. *Let her be well, please*, I pray. She's the last caring adult in our lives.

Mameh isn't at the *heim* when we return, or the next day either. On the seventh afternoon, nearly crazy with fear and anguish at the thought she might have been killed, as she's never been gone so long before, I look under Mameh's and my communal mattress. All the money, as well as the silver candlesticks, has vanished. The clothing and *maquillage* that Mameh always kept in a box under the bed have disappeared too. I gasp. She isn't dead. She made her escape while we were all out or asleep. She couldn't bear the responsibility of being with us a second longer. That there's not a single belonging of hers left except the old suitcase is bad enough. But to take the money that was for all of us to live on, to leave us without means, without a parent's care and protection? I can't believe it even of Mameh.

Thinking back a day or two later, I realize she planned to make an exit stage left all along. She was just waiting till she had enough saved to live comfortably, and that's why she welcomed New Oma, old and frail though she is, into our family — so there'd be *someone* to look after us after Mameh had gone. She must have been doing practice runs when she disappeared for a day here, two days there. I can't believe that even she would do something so flagrantly unfair, so unethical. For days I'm so stupefied by her behaviour that I can't sleep and can hardly get out of bed. I drag myself up to use the bucket, then roll myself back into my blanket again.

During this awful time, which is akin to mourning, Izo and I become friends again. Of course, she always thought we were, even though I secretly knew that we weren't. But after all, I conclude, it isn't her fault that Yoshi kissed her cheek. It isn't her fault that she's crazy about his dancing fingers and magic tricks. Who wouldn't be?

I tell Izo I'm sick and ask her to take Lotty to school. When I don't attend for the third day in a row, she asks Lotty the real reason for my absence. I'm not sure how Lotty responded, but this evening Izo came from her corner of the *heim* to mine, to visit, to commiserate, and to give me a barbecued pork bun, which she'd purloined from a Chinese vendor, and which of course isn't kosher. I can't eat it, not because it's *treif* — not kosher — but because I'm so upset that food chokes me. Close to hysterical, I tell her I'll have to leave school without obtaining my international baccalaureate. It's the final blow to my dreams, but I need to look after Lotty and New Oma. She pats my hand, promises better times, and goes away saying she's saddened by my plight.

Yoshi visits next, having outwitted the rabbi yet again. "Just think about it. Now the JJRS has some real work to do."

"Which is?"

"Which is finding your mother. It's time for the JJRS to help you, young woman. 'When sorrows come, they come not single spies, but in battalions,'" he quotes in English.

"Thank you very much, that's very helpful," I say sarcastically.

"It's Shakespeare," he points out, afraid to meet my eyes.

"I know. It's in *Hamlet*. Studied the play in class and also read it in German."

"It can be very comforting to realize that others have problems."

"You call your quote comforting? Hamlet ends up *dead*. Just go away."

He lingers, his hands rising in protest.

"Right now."

"I'll come back in a couple of days. Hopefully you'll be in a better frame of mind. In the meantime, if you need me, stick a message on the windowpane." He leaves through that same window, saying that because I don't care about him, he's going to defenestrate himself.

"We're on the ground floor, Yoshi. Unless you fall onto a pointed iron railing, which we don't happen to have at the *heim*, you're unlikely to hurt yourself." But I can't help laughing at his melodramatic antics.

"What does def-f-fenestrastrate mean?" asks Lotty.

"Defenestrate. It's an English word Yoshi likes to use to get his way. It means fall or be pushed out of a window."

"I'm going to defrenestistake my Mimi dolly."

"Good idea, Lotty. I'm tired of sewing her up every time she loses an eye. We're running out of buttons. I'm tired of Yoshi, too. Maybe they can look after each other."

"A good boy, Freda, a very good boy. Don't throw away his friendship so easily," says New Oma. She has listened quietly to my whole conversation with Yoshi. As is her habit, she didn't intervene. After a minute or two she adds, "You go back to school ... get your certificate. Will go tomorrow and find work."

"What kind of work?"

"Cleaning, washing clothes maybe."

"Don't be *meshuga*, New Oma. You can't possibly do that. It'll kill you. As it is you're saving all your food for Lotty and me."

"I eat plenty."

"Rubbish. You're getting thinner and thinner. You wouldn't have the strength to wash clothes or clean. In future, you walk Lotty to school and back so we both know she's safe. For better or worse, going out to work is now my department. I'll make enough money to feed us all."

CHAPTER 15

It's raining, a harsh, violent downpour, signalling the beginning of spring and the long, hot rainy season that precedes the sweltering summer. But it's not as hot yet as it will soon be. I've tramped all over the International Settlement and the French Concession, looking for someone to take me on, after informing the headmistress I wouldn't be coming back to the school. Shocked, she remonstrated with me, told me I was her best student. But I knew what I had to do. "I hope to come back when things are sorted out," I said. But I'm afraid that will never happen. My dreams of attending university have already vanished in a column of smoke.

"Don't give up," she said. "I'll tutor you at home when and if you have the time. You'll have a bright future after this damn war is over."

I'm finding it difficult to believe that I'll have any sort of future at all.

My boots are sodden and cracked. My coat won't button anymore; it's too skimpy to cover my blouse and skirt, which feel lined with lead because they're soaked. My skirt flaps against my legs like a dying fish. I grind my teeth in frustration. Oh, for an umbrella like the Chinese carry. That would keep me at least half dry. As it is, I'm sure that even if shopkeepers have vacancies, they won't give a job to me; half-drowned, braids drenched enough to wring out, I must look like a ghoul. Meanwhile, clouds lumber across the sky like huge black bears, lit by lightning, growling that there'll soon be even harsher rain. The streets are full of Japanese and Nazis in uniform. I shrink from them, endeavouring to pass unnoticed.

Trudging through ever narrower and dirtier alleys where the International Settlement meets its seamier side, Hongkew, I'm wondering what possessed me to come out looking for employment in this filthy weather on these filthy streets. As I turn a corner, I see before me a sign advertising the tawdry building behind it: *Green Lily Café*. The name has a familiar ring to it. I say it out loud. I shout it into the air before grimacing. Two Japanese soldiers, rushing through the alley to get out of the downpour, turn to stare at me. One points to the side of his head and makes a circular motion with his finger as if I'm insane. Perhaps I am. But I suddenly remember where I know the name from: "I work at the Green Lily Café," Mameh said not too long ago, finally letting me in on her secret. "It's a respectable establishment." Oh, right!

I creep inside, where of course it doesn't look respectable at all. The chairs and tables are scratched and stained; there's a rickety stage on which two scantily dressed women are lined up, ready to come down and dance with anyone who gives them a ticket. The members of the band are knocking back liquor and smoking.

This isn't a café, at least not the kind I've known in the past, where wealthy women accompanied by teacup-sized dogs wear flowery dresses, drink coffee or hot chocolate, and eat pastries, cake, and other delicacies. The Green Lily is a bar, and looks to be a disreputable one. At this hour it's almost empty. There are just two Chinese men sitting to the right of me, playing a game of mahjong, and a Nazi officer propping up the bar. I shiver with fear when I see him, but don't retreat. The barkeeper is swishing a dirty cloth over the counter. Everyone ignores me.

"Does Malka Isen work here?" I say to no one in particular. The band strikes up as I speak, and the girls start to dance with each other. They look like windup dolls, moving like automatons, gyrating freakishly, clacking their high heels on the floor of the stage. Their eyes closed, they've clearly retreated into their own private world.

I shout the same question again, this time to the barman. He opens a door at the back of the bar and relays my message. A brawny man, possibly the owner, appears. "'Oo wants to know?" he asks in English.

"Freda Isen. I'm her daughter."

"Your ma's not 'ere, girly. She ain't worked at the Green Lily in weeks."

I sigh. "D'you know where she went?"

"Prob'ly gone off wiv some bloke. It 'appens all the time. But after leaving me in the lurch the way she did, she wouldn't dare show her face 'ere again." He flexes his arm muscles and displays his teeth, many of which are rotten. I shrink back. Surely he can't be as vicious as he looks. "Believe me," he says, straightening his face, "you're better off wivout 'er."

"I see." Heart-heavy, I begin to walk out.

"Oy, Fried Rice or Freda Iceberg or wha'ever your name is, come back. 'Ow old are you?"

"Sixteen," I lie. Could there be a job for me at the Green Lily Café? Mameh said there was. Would I want it? Not for a scintilla of a second, but beggars can't be choosers, as Tateh used to say when I refused to eat my sauerkraut. On the other hand, when I was forced to eat it, I threw it back up.

"Wot languages can you gab in?"

"English — as you can hear — some French and Mandarin from school. German and Yiddish from home. A bit of Chinese Wu from the streets, and a few words of Japanese."

"Good. Our reg'lars speak lots of diff'rent languages. Your ma's left me anover girl short just when I bin looking for a few new faces, fresh flesh, you might say."

Ugh! He makes me feel like an eel, slimy but still slithering. "Well, I ..."

"Girls tend to come and go 'ere, for all sorts of reasons. I bet you'll polish up real nice when you dry out. Your ma's job is yours if you want it."

"Well, I ..."

"Find yourself a'evening dress and some 'igh 'eels, cut off your braids and fluff up your 'air, redden your lips, be prepared to work long hours, and dance wiv our customers as long as they 'ave money for tickets. Goin' upstairs wiv 'em ain't mandet'ry. Mind you, though, you'll earn a lot more moolah — as the Yanks say — if you do. Start Sunday night at eight."

I seem to have found myself a job. Or rather, a job has found me. I rush back through the rain, my boots squelching in puddles, to tell New Oma and Lotty — despite misgivings that are curdling the long-ago breakfast in my stomach — that it's unlikely we'll starve. New Oma shakes her head as she towels my sopping hair. Lotty shrieks with happiness. "B-buy me a sugar mouse," she yells. "A pink one."

"I will, promise, just as soon as I get paid."

The next day, Yoshi and Izo come calling. I convene a meeting of the JJRS in a basement corner of the *heim* to ask them to help me find Mameh. I give them all the clues I have, which aren't many. I honestly don't know why we should search for her. She doubtless wouldn't return if any of us found her, has made her position quite clear. Still, I can't give up, not yet, anyhow. My heart is too bruised. In return for Yoshi's and Izo's help in the search, I'll assist them in stealing food from the Japanese Army. I tell them about the Green Lily Café. They both look shaken, but Yoshi pats my shoulder and kisses my cheek as he leaves.

"I'm sorry you have to do that, although it does sound like an adventure. I'll share my lipstick with you," says Izo, unrolling it from her handkerchief. A day later, she produces a pale blue gown with sequins and, after asking my foot size, a pair of strappy high heels. She makes me practice walking in them so I don't trip. I do trip, more than once, and we giggle together. Though my knees are scraped and stinging, I'd never admit it. It would be too humiliating. And because Izo's now a fairy godmother who's waved her wand to get me the ball gown and glass slippers I need, I'm certainly not going to ask her where she got them. The only thing missing is a Prince Charming.

CHAPTER 16

I have taken on Mameh's old job. Every day I paint my mouth with Izo's blood-orange lipstick; in our shard of a mirror I look like a vampire. Stopping every now and then at work, I reveal my suspenders in order to straighten my seams, just as the other girls do and Mameh did. I'm a quick learner.

I speak to patrons of the Green Lily in an alluring way, or at least as close to alluring as I can get, though I'm sure I sound ridiculous. I take orders and set drinks and meals on tables. I steal some of the food left on plates for New Oma and Lotty after my shift is over. It will only get thrown out if I don't.

Many of the men stink of stale sweat, cigarettes, and liquor. I hate being close to them. Their reek rubs off on me, just as it did on Mameh. I see now that the nasty odours she brought home likely originated with her sweaty customers.

Since New Oma altered it, complaining and tut-tutting all the while, I wear the same type of glitzy gown that Mameh wore. I totter around in peep-toed high heels that are almost identical to hers, and wear silk stockings that are the kind that she swore at as she was putting them on. Although I want to go on hating her for forcing me in her absence to become her double, what we Germans call a doppelgänger, I'm beginning, despite the ever-present tangle of anger in my gut, to feel a dark, disturbing sympathy for her. The weight of all our lives rested on her shoulders, just as it rests now on mine. If I find her I'll be sure to let her know that though I adamantly refused before, I'd help her support our little family. But I'd want the money and candlesticks back first.

In my time off, I limp, exhausted, around the International Settlement and the French Concession, both of which are far more expensive to live in than Hongkew. I search for Mameh unsuccessfully, realizing that she might be holed up behind some door that she doesn't open when I knock. She might be just a few feet away, separated from me only by a flimsy wall. Since Mameh had said on numerous occasions that if we could ever get out of the *heim* the French Concession would be the place to live, that's where I concentrate my search. She would fit right in here. And so would I, I realize with a dull pain. No dead bodies littering the streets, no vendors screaming their wares, no filth. Instead there are wide, calm avenues shaded by perfumed trees, expensive houses, and beautiful shops and cafés. Oh, to escape the *heim* and live somewhere clean and quiet! There's even a clock and watch shop on a peaceful corner: The Bell Chime.

As I step inside I'm greeted by the familiar tinkling of clocks chiming the quarter hour. In the past, when Tateh brought them home, they annoyed me. Now they sound like angels singing, like the music of the spheres. I'd do anything to leave the café and work for the owner, Moshe Rubin, whose name is painted in red letters on the shop door. I ask in German if it would be possible. I tell him my Tateh had a store just like his, and taught me how to mend and clean both clocks and watches.

Herr Rubin, switching to Yiddish and dropping a small screw from a clock he's taking apart, says he can't afford to hire me; but he takes my name and the address of the *heim* just in case his assistant leaves or business picks up. "It would make a nice change to have a member of staff who knows what she's doing," he says with a crooked smile. Grey-haired and a little hunched over, he looks kind and fatherly, and he calls me *maidel*, just as New Oma does. I cross my fingers, hoping his assistant will go work somewhere else or everyone will suddenly want a new watch or a mended clock so he needs more assistance. But for the moment I must stay on at the Green Lily, serving, dancing, and fighting off men's creepy hands.

One early morning before dawn, on my way back to the *heim* from work, the pulse in my throat explodes, and my legs feel so weak I'm afraid I'll pass out. Someone is following me! Though I'm faint, I manage to quicken my step. I don't shake whoever it is. "Go away," I scream in both Mandarin and English. "Yoshi, if you're playing one of your tricks, stop it right now."

No reply. I scream again, frightened for my life. A moment later, a young Chinese boy creeps from the shadows, holding out his begging bowl. Even in the purplish light, I can see his arms and legs are sticks. "Please, food," he says. He's speaking Wu, as many Shanghai Chinese do, not Mandarin. Thank God he's not a thief or a thug! Just a starving street boy. After I slow my breath and recover my balance, I take a closer look at him. He stands quietly on the street, his eyes dead, seemingly with little expectation of anything. I feel a terrible sorrow for him, especially as he doesn't ask for money, as most of the professional beggars do. Money can buy anything, including alcohol and drugs, common in Shanghai. Food can only be for eating, so he must be desperate. I give him a little of what I'm bringing to Lotty and New Oma. After that night I need to pilfer more, as he meets me after almost every shift, bowl outstretched. His name, he tells me, is Song, which I find poetic and charming. He lives on the streets. I simply cannot deny him food that helps keep him alive, and I thrill to see him grow stronger. He has become a secret piece of my extended family.

Sometimes, when I'm not too tired, I linger to talk to him. I feel an instant kinship when he tells me his mother and father are both dead, since I don't know whether one or even both of my parents have died. I learn so much of Song's Wu dialect that I become fluent in it, and he learns Yiddish and a little English from me. How strange: A Chinese boy who speaks Yiddish! A Yiddishe *maidel* who speaks Wu! Could I introduce him to the JJRS? Even though he's not Jewish, he would almost certainly consider the Japanese his enemies, and he might even feel enough loyalty to me to join.

Still, I have to be careful, both about food and our plans for the Japanese, because the café boss always appears to be watching me. I don't think he's yet discovered my meagre thefts, though I come slim and leave fat, the food hidden in a bag under my dress. He probably wouldn't care, as it's bound for the garbage anyway, but I can't be sure, as he's so unpredictable.

There are other matters, especially regarding the Japanese and the Nazis, that he definitely does care about. In a rough voice he commands me to behave like the other girls, to joke with both our Japanese and Nazi clients. "They could kill us in a moment," he growls, "so cuddle up to the guys you dance wiv. Go furver. Tease more." Ugh. Why in the world would I want to do that? But his black piano-key teeth are bared when he tells me off for keeping my distance from what he calls the "Jap and Kraut barflies." He resembles a dangerous animal closing in for the kill. His monstrous glare and decayed teeth frighten me into submission.

"If you quit like your ma I'll come after you, see if I don't," he warns one drunken night. "I ain't aiming to lose anover girl unless it's to the Grim Reaper."

I'm petrified, remembering the feeling of being followed in the shadows. One day, doubtless, the boss or a customer will do something brutal to me. It wouldn't be out of place at the Green Lily, where bloody battles break out almost every day, so ferocious sometimes that the floor runs red. I've even seen the owner himself go at someone with a knife when the man wouldn't pay his bill. In the wake of that attack I cleave my tongue to the roof of my mouth, stay *stum*, and submit to the boss's demands. I make sure I don't tell anyone about how nightmarish my job is. I don't even tell Yoshi. He would insist I quit, but I have a family to feed. There's no other choice but to continue there. Or at least, if there *is* another choice, I haven't yet found it.

"We haven't seen your mother, though we've searched all over. Sorry," Yoshi says many weeks later, having managed to escape the *yeshiva* just as I'm going out the *heim* door for my shift at the Green Lily.

"That's all right. I didn't expect you to. I haven't seen her either." She's been gone at least two months. After work or on my day off I go from house to house asking. I patrol the streets. I visit bars and restaurants in the International Settlement and French Concession. I know Mameh well enough to realize she wouldn't remain in Hongkew. "There's not a trace of her. She obviously doesn't want to be found."

"To be honest, I don't know why you're still looking. You're better off without her. She'll never give you the approval you're wanting. You can't make her care for you," he says bluntly.

"Thank you, Dr. Freud."

He laughs. "I miss you. I haven't seen you in what seems like ages. How's your job going?"

"Fine," I lie.

"I'll come and visit you at your workplace soon. See what you're up to."

"No, don't. Please don't."

"Why not? What's the matter with you, Freda? "

"Nothing is the matter with me. Just don't visit, that's all. The boss is fiercely against us having guests. He fired a girl last week for bringing her boyfriend in." Though I hate to lie to Yoshi, I'm doing it again. Telling frightful lies is becoming easier and easier as time passes.

"Very well." His voice is grim. "But you look frightened. And you're trembling."

"I'm not frightened; I'm just cold."

"Cold when summer's coming? It's about eight hundred degrees. How can you be cold?"

I ignore his questions. "Listen, try to arrange a meeting of the JJRS during the day sometime, when I'm not working, and then we can discuss where we're at."

"Very well," he says again, his face bleak. He disappears down an alley just as two Japanese officers emerge from it.

Groups of Japanese people are common sights on the streets. They are our overlords. When off-duty, many of them patronize the Green Lily or other bars. They tend to be polite and formal, very different from many of our other customers, at least until they get drunk. I've heard enough from others to have no illusions about what they'd do if I displeased them, especially if they've been drinking. They'd shoot a man in the head as soon as look at him. The Nazis are the same. They all seem to be massing, which is, of course, incredibly upsetting.

I often serve drinks to large tables full of Japanese or Nazi soldiers, and have frequently danced with them when they hand me their tickets. I have no choice, and besides, what I'm doing is useful. I smile and joke with the Nazis, as commanded by my boss. The Japanese don't know I'm good at languages and learned Japanese on the streets. So I can listen to the soldiers with impunity, without fear I'll be accused of eavesdropping.

One evening, as I serve them drinks, I get wind of a shipment of food and ammunition due in at the Whangpoo wharf. I strive to look blank-faced so the two officers talking won't suspect me of understanding their conversation. This is information I'll need to pass on to Yoshi and Izo as soon as possible. We must try to do — no, we must *absolutely* do — something about it.

"We'll feed the poorer refugees and Chinese like Song, a boy I've met, and give the ammo to the Underground if we can find where they hide it," I tell my two comrades of the JJRS.

Izo is painting her nails. "I'll do yours next," she promises.

"Are you talking to me?" asks Yoshi, fluttering both his eyelashes and his fingers.

"No, stupid. Put your hands down. I'm talking to Freda."

"I hate nail varnish," I say. "Can I bring Song with me? He's loyal, and he'll be a great help."

"No," says Yoshi.

"Sure," counters Izo.

"I'll take that as a yes."

"When is the shipment arriving?" asks Yoshi, changing the subject.

"Don't know. Soon. I'll find out," I promise, sure I'll hear it spoken of again at the Green Lily, which seems to have become the unofficial headquarters of the Japanese.

"Good. You're right in what you say, Freda." Yoshi smiles. "We'll steal from the rich to give to the poor. Like Janosik, the Polish outlaw."

"Like Schinderhannes," I counter, a German soldier. "He stole from the rich too, but I'm not sure he gave to the poor."

"Ha! Just like a German!" Yoshi looks through his long, girlish eyelashes while accomplishing a triple finger manoeuvre that produces a Chinese cookie. It would leave my hands in knots if I tried to copy it.

"Agreed," says Izo. "I will find some camouflage clothes. Dark green ruffled jacket and cock hat, with perhaps a muffler if it's cold. Long, dark skirt. Black high heels like a real spy. Can't wait to do a proper heist. It'll be fun."

"This isn't a fashion parade, Izo," I remonstrate. "You have to get serious. What we're doing is illegal, and I dread to think what might happen if the Japanese catch us."

"Except ..." Yoshi pauses as if about to announce the end of the war. "I feel confident we can get in and out of there with no problem. I've joined the Thirteenth Rovers."

"The what?" asks Izo, her green eyes round as a bush baby's.

"The Thirteenth Rovers. It's like the British Boy Scouts, only it's for Jewish refugees. It'll help me practice for our work in the JJRS."

"Indubitably," say I, trying out a new English word I learned at school. I'm not sure of its meaning, but it seems to fit securely into our conversational jigsaw, which consists of puzzle pieces of English, Yiddish, and German. "I'll join too."

"And me." Izo grins.

"Don't be dopey. It's only for boys."

"How stupid that it's only for boys. Girls are just as brave, if not braver," says Izo.

"No doubt." Yoshi awards me the cookie, magicking up another for Izo when she pouts. He pulls a Chinese sparkler from his pocket, lights it, and whirls it around. "You never know when a match will come in handy!"

"I love the sparks, and the pinpoints of colour they leave in their wake." Izo is waltzing around as if we're in a ballroom.

Leaning toward Yoshi, I snatch the sparkler and stamp it out. "Stop joking around. We must strategize immediately," I say sternly, sounding like a German commandant.

"Indubitably!" Yoshi winks. He's mocking me. I don't like it.

"Get serious. You and Izo are driving me crazy."

"*Ja, ja*, Fredaaa!" he sings. His eyes unreadable, the colour of underwater pearls, he performs a Nazi salute before twirling around and hopping away like a sparrow. He and Izo are acting as if everything is a joke, which is inexcusable considering the danger of the situation. They are playing around like young children while the frequent threats from disembodied voices on the radio and the reconnaissance flights that split the sky like lightning are warnings of what's to come. The piling up of weapons and supplies are evil and frightening omens. It is a sign that we will soon all be in danger: my family — or at least, what's left of them — my friends, and all the inhabitants of the three-cornered city. The night sky will crack open with bombers as they train their deadly sights on Shanghai.

The moon drops into hiding, and the stars start to appear like sequins in the dusky sky. It may be a message from God, but how am I to decipher it?

"The rest is silence," Yoshi yells from behind a wall. He hops back and performs one last balletic whirl, falling flat on his back and pedalling his legs in the air. Izo bends over him, snorting with laughter. I turn my back on their stupidity and rush away, annoyed with both of them and late for work.

CHAPTER 17

Half awake, late in the afternoon, I keep still and quiet, not willing to drag myself out of bed, and make myself ready for the job that is so distasteful to me. Listening to the chatter of the other refugees in the *heim*, I fall back to sleep even as I'm telling myself I have to get up.

A door opens in front of me, letting in golden light and the aromatic scent of roses and lilacs. Bees buzz, and cows make their mournful sound. I'm at my old Oma's house in the country!

I rush through the door, but cannot find any trace of Oma's garden, of her climbing roses or lilacs, her beehives or cowsheds. Instead, a tangle of nightmarish images assails my brain: Tateh dead in a camp, Mameh leaving, Hans glaring at me — not across a street but a raging river in which boats are capsizing, refugees drowning. Old Oma dead, New Oma dying. Starved corpses on the streets of Hongkew lying in grotesque attitudes, their eyes wide in horror. All of them rise and advance toward me, their arms outstretched like gnarled, thorn-tipped branches. Closing in, tall as trees, their twiggy hands begin to pull at me. Their knotty mouths open in toothless grins. They shriek like wild beasts. Terrified, I run back through the door and try to shake the spectres off, sleep still clutching me in its tight embrace.

"Is there any food?" asks Lotty, waking me up.

"Nothing much till the next … *heim* meal." There is a pause. New Oma's breath is laboured after walking Lotty back from school. "In the kitchen."

"Ugh. W-worm soup and bread hard as a plank after us lining up for hours."

"There, there. There's still a little of what Freda brought home this morning … Will take you to the market soon as she gets paid."

I sigh with relief. Life in the *heim* is horrible, but not half as gruesome as life in the camps, or even life in my dreams. I'm sweating like a pig, so I wipe my underarms with a damp rag before dressing for work. As I leave the *heim*, the dreams don't fade.

Someone is walking behind me. I turn around. It's a man with his hat brim drawn down over his eyes and, despite the stuffy evening, a muffler covering his nose and lips. I've seen him before at the Green Lily, and he seems oddly familiar. Is he a friend or enemy? I can't figure it out, especially as he never takes off his hat. The street is crowded in any case. There's nothing he can do to me here without risking prison. Still, I quicken my pace. He follows me into the café and sits down in the farthest corner, his usual place, reading a French newspaper. Between the paper and the wide hat brim, there's not much to be seen of his face.

A noisy group of Nazis sit in front of him, toasting one another with beer steins and singing the Horst Wessel song:

The street is free for the brown battalions,
The street is free for the Storm Troopers.
Millions, full of hope, look up at the swastika;

The day breaks for freedom and for bread.
Their voices breathe terror into my bones.

Three Japanese officers seat themselves at the next table. I try to listen carefully as I serve them in case they mention the date of their incoming shipment of food and equipment. But I can't hear what they're saying because of the racket. After the Horst Wessel song ends, the band strikes up. This, however, doesn't stop the Nazis. Now they're singing:

The rotten bones are trembling,
Of the World before the War.
We have smashed this terror,
For us a great victory!

I bite my lip to stop myself from shouting out. A Nazi grabs my hand and puts a ticket into it, almost dislocating my shoulder as he pulls me up to the stage to dance with him. My gorge rises, but he's so drunk he can only manage a few steps before falling on the floor and being dragged back to his chair by two of his comrades.

One of the Nazis has his back to me. His white-blond hair, the nape of his neck, and his long, wide hands are reminiscent of Hans. I chide myself for still thinking of him after all these years; but finally seeing his profile as he speaks in a low tone into a comrade's ear, I shudder with excitement and fear. It *is* Hans, I'm almost certain of it. A grown-up Hans in a grey Nazi uniform, but Hans all the same. If things were bad before, they're immeasurably worse now. Telling the boss I'm too sick to work, I feel a tremendous wave of nausea before rushing through the door and throwing up on someone's shoes. It's the mystery man from the Green Lily. He's followed me.

"I'm so sorry," I say.

"No problem, I'll walk you home," he says. "These shoes are old anyhow, and much too big. I took them from a dead man's feet. Plenty more where they came from." He doffs his hat and bows, kissing my hand. Then he takes out a handkerchief and wipes off his shoes before steering me away from the puddle of vomit. It's Yoshi, the master of disguise! "I followed you here last week to see where you work and to take care of you if things got dangerous."

"I can look after myself, thanks."

"Right. That's why you were throwing up on my shoes, not to mention the road."

"It's not for the reasons you might think."

"Freda, not to make too much of it, but you look like you've seen a ghost."

"Don't be an idiot." I even *sound* like Mameh now. But he's right. I have seen a ghost, a spectre from my distant past.

"As if I haven't realized the cause of your sickness. It's those Nazis, singing their cursed songs."

"Yes," I reply quickly. "Yes, you're right. They remind me of Kristallnacht and of the black and white newsreels of how our part of Berlin looked afterwards."

"Don't worry, they have no power over you or any of us here in Shanghai. It's said that Hitler wanted us all killed, he even sent over material to make gas chambers, but in the end the Japanese wouldn't oblige." He pauses for a second. "But more important to our efforts right now, I also found out the date of the shipment by listening in to the talk that went on between the Japanese officers."

"Really?"

"Yes. While you were dancing around the stage with that drunken Nazi, looking like Cinderella at the Führer's ball,

I found out it's tomorrow. So we should plan to go discover it in two days or so."

I'm glad to change the subject. "Great. That will be my evening off. We have to let Izo and Song know, and tell them where and what time to meet."

"How about twelve at night in front of the Ward Street prison? It seems apt enough."

"Fine. I'll tell Izo in the morning. Here comes Song now, though tonight I have no food for him."

"No problem." Yoshi pulls three almond cookies from his hat and, with an elaborate bow, gives them to Song, who manages a timid but wide grin.

"Thank you," he says in Yiddish.

"You're welcome," Yoshi replies in Wu.

Despite my despair, I laugh at both of them. "Give me one for Lotty," I ask, "if you have any left."

"Indubitably." He winks. "I have a never-ending supply. Here you are." Enchanting as always, he magicks up another cookie from his hat, then another, and another. "That's for Lotty, for your New Oma if she still has teeth to chew it, and for you when you don't feel as sick."

The door of the Green Lily flies open. The Nazis are on the street. Still singing, they push by us, giving one another playful punches and prancing around like boxers. They take no notice of us, thank goodness. They behave as though we're mere obstacles in their path. Suddenly a dark-haired officer, much older than the others, wallops Song hard in the belly. Song doubles over and groans. I wrap my arm around him to keep him from falling. The officer moves on.

In the dark pre-dawn, Yoshi's face is paler than the waning moon as he stares angrily at the soldiers. They are lit by the bluish light that streams from the café's windows, so I see them clearly. And I was right all along: the blond soldier is Hans, it is! I recognize the birthmark on his forehead, his honey-amber eyes, and tremble in fear and longing. What will I do if he turns up at the Green Lily again? Sooner or later he's bound to recognize me. What will I say? What might he?

CHAPTER 18

A door opens into the past: Hans swings around a corner. I'm unable to banish him after seeing him at the Green Lily. Hans and I lived next door to each other and were the greatest of pals through our early childhood, though he was a couple of years older than me. We skipped stones into a nearby river together. We played marbles. I still carry one in my coat pocket, a marvel of translucent blues and greens. He helped me with my science homework, all the while teasing me mercilessly. He soon found I could give as good as I got.

Hans and I went on secret missions, armed with cheese sandwiches and sauerkraut. He ate all the sauerkraut because I detested it. But when I was eight Hans told me the most terrible news: his parents had forbidden him to speak to me anymore, as I was Jewish, and his family were going to move to a more "wholesome" area, as he put it. I guess he meant to an area without Jews. His family was wealthy and could afford to do so. He had it on good authority, he said, sounding like his father — a commander in the Great War many years before we were both born — that the Jewish quarter would soon be cordoned off. It was a hard time to sell, so his parents had decided to lease their home to a Jewish family, the Grundmans, as there were no Christian takers. The Grundmans had nowhere to go after their own landlord pitched them out. It was an unlucky time and an unlucky house, all things considered.

Hans also received a letter instructing him to join the Hitler Youth organization. I was devastated at the loss of our friendship, and thought he must be distressed by it too. He was obliged to do what his parents and the government told him to, after all, even though, I believed, he must have struggled, at least in his mind, against their orders.

How wrong could I be? "I'm honoured to be asked to join the Hitler Youth," he told me proudly, his chest puffed up like a turkey's. "It's my first step toward becoming an officer in the Führer's army. Just like my father, who is about to take up arms again."

"Against who?"

"Whoever. War is in the air. The world is ours for the taking!" He raised his arm in a Nazi salute. I stepped back, appalled.

His family moved on, quickly replaced on the street by the Grundmans. It was as if Hans had never lived there. I didn't see him again. At least, I didn't see him until one day I noticed a bunch of Hitler Youth boys on the pavement. They were walking toward me, sniggering and smoking. They attempted to march but were too disorganized, probably drunk. I held my ground, terrified that if I turned and ran, they would chase after me.

"Out of the way, ugly Jew girl," one of them roared when he reached me. "Look at that Jewy nose, fat as a pumpkin." He threw his cigarette butt in the dirt. Someone else began to push by. It was Hans! He had a small brown birthmark on his forehead that was an unmistakable identifier. A swastika was pinned to his shirt. His almost white hair was cut so short I could see his scalp, shining pink through the blond. Cowering, I kept my head down after recognizing him, to avoid meeting his eyes. My legs felt boneless. I was slippery with sweat. I could smell my own stink.

One of the boys spat at me. Another pressed me against a wall, trying to push his hand between my knees.

"Get away," I screamed. "Leave me alone."

"I could shoot you if I wanted to, just like this." He held a pretend gun to my head and pulled its imaginary trigger. "Pow, pow, you're dead." His Hitler Youth comrades hooted with laughter and slapped their legs.

All but Hans. "That's enough," he cried.

"Wassa matter, Hansy boy? She's only a stinking Jew. Soon we'll be rid of them all." But the youth rejoined the others, and they goose-stepped down the street without glancing back. They were singing a Nazi song in raucous voices, as they lifted their arms in the Nazi salute:

We'll go on marching
Even if everything shatters
Today Germany hears us
Tomorrow the world!

Hans too sang the song. He was just another disgusting Hitlerite, another anti-Semite, no different from the others, except when he stopped his comrade from tormenting me. But it wasn't enough, not nearly enough, especially after he joined in that Nazi song.

All my romantic notions of us being a couple when we grew up died on the street that day. How could I think I knew someone so well when in truth I didn't know him at all? My knees started to buckle; it was hard to get home.

I tried to stop thinking of him. Every time he invaded my brain, I'd do my best to bury him under memories of the latkes we'd had for dinner or the math problems Tateh gave me to solve when I was banned from school. I built make-believe structures to keep Hans out, held his head under spectral pools of water, tried to stop him from resurfacing. But banished from my waking mind, he goose-stepped through my dreams. I'd wake with feelings of profound sadness or anger, aware that I needed to bury the memory of him all over again. Though I finally managed to submerge my thoughts of Hans, that glimpse of him on the street tonight had brought him back into screaming focus.

CHAPTER 19

Two nights later, after going to bed early, I rise when both New Oma and Lotty appear to be asleep. New Oma is certainly sleeping, as she's lying on her back with both eyes shut and her mouth open, snoring, and Lotty is breathing easily, with an occasional snort. I slip into trousers and a black sweater, much too big, that I traded for a little food from the café, but carry my shoes in my hand, though there's really no reason to muffle my footsteps. The room is a cacophony of the high cries and low moans of those dreaming, and a snoring cantata in C major performed by many of the other refugees.

A small torch, bought on the street, lights my way. As I leave our little cubicle, Lotty turns over and sits up. "Where you going so late, Freda?"

"Work."

"Don't be s-silly. You never go to work in the middle of the night. You go much, much, earlier. And you're not wearing the right clothes."

"All right. If it's any of your business, Fräulein Nosy, I'm really going to meet Yoshi at a midnight party in the International

Settlement. We have things to talk about."

"What things?"

"Adult things."

"Is he your boyfriend?"

"Of course not."

Lotty sighs. "Good! I love Yoshi. I want to m-marry him when I grow up. He does card tricks and brings me sweeties. Let me come too!"

"Not in a million years. Face the wall and go back to sleep." I hear her protest feebly before she lowers her head and turns back over.

"Spoilsport," she hisses. But I know her well enough. She'll be fast asleep in a moment or two, Mimi, whom she's decided not to defenestrate, clutched in her paw.

I pull on my shoes and meet Izo outside the *heim* as arranged earlier today. We are standing in a small circle of light that is radiating from the torch. So that we aren't apprehended and questioned, I click it off. As my eyes become accustomed to the dark, I see that Izo's wearing a long skirt and high heels, as she recently promised — or rather warned — she would. She is spilling out of her blouse, which is too tight. Her lipstick is a red-blue gash in the gibbous moon's crescent. "I'm here," she pants, her weight compromising her need to hurry. "Where are we meeting Yoshi?"

"We're not meeting him anywhere unless and until you change your outfit. It's not a soirée we're engaged in, but a secret mission. Your shoes are the worst, clacking along the street. If you don't wear your flats, they'll give us all away. And for God's sake wash that crap off your face."

"You use it often enough," she pouts as, stung by my words, she begins to argue. She is going to tread in Mata Hari's footsteps. She is going to become the most famous female spy ever. She is going to rescue us all from the tyranny of the Japanese and the Nazis. She can do whatever she wants to. I'm not the boss of her. And on and on. Her voice rises to a wail. I never really realized before what a total idiot she is. The word *idiot* rankles, bringing with it unpleasant memories.

"Quiet. I don't have time for any of this. Either you go and change right now, or I'm leaving you behind. I'll give you two minutes." She clip-clops away, still arguing, her pencil–thin skirt an impediment to her steps. The clatter of her shoes infuriates me. I feel an angry flush rising from my neck to the top of my head. I seem to be reprimanding everyone tonight; my brain is clotted with fear and rage.

"I won't be back," she says. She means it. After several minutes of waiting in the gathering fog, I set off to the prison without her. A forbidding building, which looms out of the grey-black mist, it has stout walls with shards of broken glass embedded in them and scattered along their tops. No one could possibly escape from it without suffering severe injury. It lights up every now and then because of a revolving floodlight, so it wasn't a good place to arrange to meet. My pulse thumps raggedly. My mouth is parched. What are we doing here? Why are we such daredevils? Will we end up in this jail?

Someone is standing behind me. I freeze at the sound of his cat-like step. I can feel his breath. In a moment the person is pirouetting his way around me. It's Yoshi, thank goodness, wearing a mask and a black cloak, not a member of the Shanghai police or the Japanese army. He's carrying a large cane. I barely recognize him in his peculiar getup, but who else would dress that way in the middle of the night, or during the day, for that matter? He taps me lightly on the shoulder. "I Zorro," he says none too quietly and with a peculiar accent. His playacting can be so annoying.

"Who the heck's Zorro?"

"I am 'eroic bandit. I 'elp oppressed peoplez and kill ze wicked ones. I carry zis big stick. Where's Izo?" he asks, shifting gears into his normal voice.

"No idea. I sent her back to change her ridiculous outfit — though in retrospect it's no more ridiculous than yours — and she hasn't reappeared. Where's Song?"

"Singing somewhere else, perhaps. Scared of what might happen. The Japanese and just about everyone else use home- less Chinese boys for target practice. So he's probably gone back to hide in the shadows, and there are just us involved in our JJRS caper."

"And m-me," says a small voice. "I followed you."

"So I see. You can't come with," I snap, close to screeching at her. "Go back to the *heim*."

Her eyes well with tears. "I can't."

"Yes, you can. Just spin around and go back the way you came. It's only a couple of minutes along the road."

"I'm s-scared."

"Were you scared coming here?"

"Nope."

"Well then."

She turns and walks away disconsolately. "I'll take her," volun- teers Yoshi. They both disappear from the edges of the prison floodlight. I instantly feel ashamed. She's my only sister, after all, perhaps the last remaining member of my family. I've vowed to myself over and over again that I'd take care of her. But tonight I'm blazing with anger: at her, at Izo, at Mameh, Hans, and even Yoshi himself, though in his characteristic way he'll make sure that she arrives home safely. He's taken the action I should have taken. But knowing him so well, I'm sure he's pacified her with candies, which he's pilfered from who knows where. And that makes me even angrier.

When he runs back, I lay into him. "Her teeth will rot from all that sugar. I bought her a sugar mouse once, and all it did was give her the most frightful toothache. You should keep your candies to yourself."

"Stop it, Freda, just stop it. I'm not surprised that Izo dropped out if you snarled at her that way. What's wrong with you?"

"Nothing."

"It's that Nazi, that pretty boy Nazi you clapped eyes on the other night that you seemed so interested in, isn't it?"

"I have no idea what you're talking about." Rather than look at him, I begin to pick at a loose thread in my black sweater.

"Of course you do. Take care to stay away from him. He may be pretty, but he bears the mark of Cain."

"Don't talk such rot," I counter, and though I know he's making sense I close my ears against it. Yoshi sounds jealous — unusual for him. And he's too perceptive, something that usually pleases me, especially when he's talking of someone else. In the present situation, though, I don't like it at all, will have to be more careful about what I say and who I look at. "He's merely someone I knew once, long, long ago. He lived near me in Berlin, and we were childhood friends."

"Friends or sweethearts?"

"Friends," I reply haughtily. "Nothing more. After all, we were children. But our friendship ended when he became a member of the Hitler Youth."

"I should hope so. Now he's a full-grown Nazi. Again, stay away from him or you might find yourself dangling from the end of a rope."

"Thanks for the warning," I say sarcastically, before burying the subject with an imaginary spade. "Where are we going?"

"To where the Japanese hid the shipment, obviously. I followed them as they moved it. I'd been tracking their movements for weeks. They'd been carousing at the Green Lily, and most were far too drunk to notice me. One, lagging behind and weaving back and forth in his drunken stupor, saw me. But before he got a chance to raise his bayonet, I bashed him on the head with this stick I've been carrying with me in case of trouble, and he fell into a faint, not knowing what hit him."

I can't believe that Yoshi would ever do anything violent. He seems so amiable and kind: "A gentle soul," New Oma once called him. But this is no time to reflect on his character. He vanishes around a dusty corner. Grabbing hold of his sleeve so I don't lose him, I follow him into a dirty alleyway lit only by the dim auras of candles still burning in the hovels around us. The inky silence is suddenly shattered by people tumbling out of a bar, women yelling and men fighting and swearing in several languages. We try to squeeze past them, but the throng is growing, reaching from one side of the alley to the other. Voices swell to a crescendo as one man stabs another, who drops like a butchered bull. As he falls, his blood spurts in an arc from his body. Some of it lands on my arm.

"You Jewed me," the stabber yells in Yu, waving the knife around and threatening to stab him again. "I want my money back." But it's too late. The victim groans, then goes quiet. His eyes are unseeing as blood continues to pour from his wound, a dark red crescent like an August moon. It stops as suddenly as it started. He's dead. The other men set upon him, punching and kicking, as if his death isn't enough punishment. They trample on his *kipa*, his face. They rifle through his pockets, finding little of any value. It spurs them to even greater violence. "What can you expect from a Jew?" says one, before running off. The others disappear too, like waters receding after a flood.

I cower against a wall, wiping the victim's blood off me as best as I can. It leaves a sticky residue on my arm and I shudder. I feel contaminated by it, unclean. Yoshi hauls me along the alley. "Come on," he whispers. "I'm sorry you saw that, I'm sorry you were stained by it, but there's no time to delay."

I whimper, terrified. "I'm scared, Yoshi."

He puts his other arm around me and half pulls, half pushes me along. "'Screw your courage to the sticking place, and we'll not fail.' Lady Macbeth. Shakespeare." As the light falters, he looks like a blind man, holding his stick in front of him, knocking it on the ground and pushing it into nooks and crevices as we go.

After a few minutes we leave the Chinese district. Once I've stopped shaking, I switch my torch back on. Its light calms me. Apart from a catfight with what sounds like a dozen cats yowling at one another and chasing around our feet, there are no further catastrophes. We're at the edge of Hongkew — Japanese territory. I've never been here before. Fog swirls around the edges of the torch's faint beam, sinister and eerie. One good thing: In this gloom, if I switch off the torch, the Japanese will never be able to find us.

CHAPTER 20

"We're here," announces Yoshi, after we've hiked for what feels like hours into the country. I've clicked off my torch. In the faint rosy glow of the eastern sky, its blush dissipating fog as dawn approaches, I can make out barn-like areas all around us, as well as barracks and tents; there's also a checkpoint, no doubt to stop civilians entering.

No one appears to be on guard. We climb over the checkpoint and into the installation. Nothing stirs.

"It's too late," I whisper, as the sky brightens. "Soon it will be morning."

"Rubbish," Yoshi whispers back. "The soldiers are sound asleep, and will sleep at least until the sun rises in an hour or so. As I said, I saw them after they carried their food and *matériel* up from the harbour — in carts. They're lazy buggers. Drink like fish at night and stay abed in the morning."

"How do you know? How can you spend all your time watching them? Don't you ever have to study?"

"The *yeshiva* threw me out," he confesses. "For continually breaking the rules. I thought they hadn't noticed."

Another shock, but we can't deal with that problem — if Yoshi views it as a problem — now. We must attend to the matter at hand. "It's too late to carry out our plans," I repeat. "Let's get away from here."

"If we lose our nerve when we're on the brink of success, there'll likely never be another chance. Have a candy."

"No." I knock his arm away. "Don't be an idiot." Again one of Mameh's favourite words! Ugh! I can't believe I said it. Why can't I stop myself? But more important, at this point I don't care if we rescue the supplies. Was it really my suggestion that we trudge out to somewhere far from our usual haunts to seize food and armaments from the Japanese army? Did I truly feel I'd be safe tramping around at night in some of the worst areas of Hongkew as well as into unknown country? And with someone who was careless enough to be expelled from the *yeshiva*? Not that I knew that till just now. Even so, I must have been out of my mind! What was I thinking? I should run back to the *heim*, climb into bed, and bury myself under my blanket till the war is over or I die, whichever comes first.

"I came back yesterday and hid a wheelbarrow behind a tree so we can carry our loot to Shanghai," declares Yoshi. "It's over here." But the wheelbarrow has been hacked to pieces. Yoshi finally looks frightened, his face paler in the starlight than I've ever seen it. His hand shakes, and he drops his stick.

Sirens suddenly begin to shriek. An enormous searchlight clicks on. It finds us fast. I'm as brain-frozen as a deer caught in headlights. We are bathed in a circle of fierce light as a Japanese officer barks out commands and half-dressed soldiers with sleep-filled eyes stream from their barracks, training their bayonets on us.

The officer is horribly close. He pulls his pistol from its holster as he moves even closer, pressing the gun to the side of

Yoshi's temple, just above his ear. I let out a moan.

"Quiet! What you doing in this place?" He speaks in a harsh mixture of bad English and worse German. I can hardly bear to look at him, in case the gun goes off suddenly, shattering Yoshi's brain.

"We're lovers, looking for a quiet place to be alone," Yoshi says, thinking faster than I can, even with a pistol to his head. "Where we stay, in the better area of Hongkew, it's so crowded that we can't get a moment's privacy. We had no idea there was an installation here."

"How you get in?"

"Over a gate. In the dark we thought it led to a farmer's field."

The officer turns to me. "Where you come from?"

"Germany," I say in German, though as a Jew I'm now stateless.

"Germany," reiterates Yoshi the Polish Jew, also in German. "I'm visiting Shanghai with my father, who's a Nazi officer. Anna's my girlfriend."

"And the wheelbarrow?"

"What wheelbarrow?" I say innocently. Apparently this is the right answer. The officer removes his pistol from Yoshi's head. The troops lower their bayonets. I take a deep, ragged breath. Yoshi gives a gusty sigh of relief.

"Germans our friends, allies. Why you dress up like that?" the officer asks Yoshi.

"We've been to a costume party. It's Halloween, or at least, it was last night. You know what Halloween is?"

The officer looks puzzled. But "Sure," he answers, though it's not October, so he obviously doesn't. He returns his gun to its holster. "What your father's name?"

"Commander Wilhelm Schmidt."

"Aha! If you children here again, I speaks your father. Understand?"

"Absolutely, sir."

"Now shoo, shoo," he says, as if we're chickens. He turns and begins to walk back to the barracks with his troops.

We scramble over the gate, race away, and don't slow down for at least a mile. Half dead from exhaustion, my legs aching as if they'll snap, I bend over, gasping for air.

"Well, that was a success," laughs Yoshi, "though we lost the wheelbarrow and it wasn't really mine."

"A success? Are you crazy? We didn't do one thing we set out to do. So much for the training of the Thirteenth Rovers!"

He twirls around before executing a Nazi salute. "Jawohl, Fräulein Freda! I vill see you home."

"Which reminds me. Where are you living now?"

"Everywhere and nowhere," Yoshi replies mysteriously.

> Over hill, over dale,
> Through bush, through briar,
> Over park, over pale,
> Through blood, through fire,
> I fall asleep just anywhere.

"Profound apologies to Shakespeare," he adds. "And to Titania's fairy. I made the last bit up."

How the heck does he know all that literary stuff? It just gushes out of him at opportune moments. As if he can hear me wondering, he bows. "I've spent a lot of time in libraries, you know. There's nothing better than a book, unless it's a wurst sandwich."

As the sun comes up, illuminating his clever face, he grins. But his paleness, which as the sun rises is even more evident, seems an omen. In a deep, dismal corner of my mind, I still picture him, brilliant youth that he is, toppled by lightning, lying dead at the Japanese officer's feet. It shall not, cannot be, I promise myself, not if I have anything to do with it.

CHAPTER 21

I am very small, riding on Tateh's shoulders, hanging onto the back of his neck like a baby monkey. We are going to a parade, Tateh tells me, with clowns, ballerinas, and elephants. Perhaps an elephant will wind its trunk around me and lift me onto its back. I have never seen a live elephant — although I've looked at a picture of one in my book — but I did once see a clown. It was at the circus, and he came and sat next to me. I was scared and started to cry. But I won't be scared again, because now I know from Mameh that a clown is just an ordinary man with a painted face. I have the best view in the world up here; if I reach up, I can touch the clouds, which are white and fluffy. Perhaps I will catch a piece of one and drop it into my pocket.

Three elephants are lumbering down the street. The ballerinas in their glittering tutus are twirling. Clowns in multicoloured costumes skip by, holding hands, as a marching band strikes up, playing a Christmas song, "O Tannenbaum." Christmas trees covered in tinsel, I notice, are now waltzing along with the ballerinas.

The clouds go black and it starts to rain. I blink. When I open my eyes the Christmas trees and ballerinas are gone. The elephants are gone. The clowns are gone. Only the band remains. It is blaring a Nazi song. Nazi battalions turn the corner and goose-step onto the street, faces clown-painted. They are just ordinary men, I tell myself. But they are yelling the words of the song:

All these hypocrites, we throw them out,
Judea leave our German house!
If the native soil is clean and pure,
We united and happy will be!

"Tateh?" But Tateh has gone too, after setting me back on the ground and leaving me on my own. The rain has changed to icy pellets of snow, and a biting wind blows. I am standing, small and alone, on the pavement. I want to run away but can't. A Nazi officer kneels beside me and, smiling, puts his pistol to my head. It is Hans. As he pulls the trigger ...

Lotty calls, "Freda, Freda, wake up right now. I need you." She has saved my life. "New Oma won't get up," cries Lotty. "She says she's too t-tired, but I can go by myself to school."

I throw off my blanket, quit my cot, and struggle to think through the half-remembered aura of my hellish dream. New Oma's eyes are closed. "New Oma?" I lift her hand. It's ice-cold; the bones are small and brittle as those of a sparrow. I turned over a small bird that was lying outside our house once, when I was a very young child. The bird was dead, but its underside was alive with maggots. I've never touched a bird since. The thought fills me with loathing. When I let New Oma's hand go, it falls back on her blanket; she doesn't rouse. Perhaps she's in a coma, or worse, dead. I break into a heavy, icy sweat. But unlike the bird, New Oma is still breathing. I hear a faint, bubbly sound when I put my ear to her chest.

Ducking under the sheet that separates us from the family in the next cubicle, I ask the woman to come. "Nothing to be done," she says, when she's seen New Oma. "The doctors won't come out for an old stick of a refugee like her, so she'll probably die soon. She looks starved. Your *family*," she sneers, before going away.

"My family what?" I call after her, baffled. But she shakes her head, obviously unwilling to be drawn into our drama. Although angry, I try to think charitably of her. Her clothes stink of mould and sweat and are many times mended. She probably has nothing to change into and no doubt has the crises of her own family to deal with, like many of the other *heim* residents. If Mameh was overwhelmed with our problems, how can I expect a stranger not to be?

So there's no one else. It's up to me. I take a tougher approach, calling New Oma's name loudly in her ear. After a minute or two, thank God, she opens her eyes. Or at least, she opens one of them. "Sorry ... Freda. Not well." She struggles to get out of bed.

"You stay there, New Oma," I say, throwing my clothes on as fast as I can. I drag the blanket from my cot, spread it over hers and tuck it in. "I'll fetch you some breakfast from the kitchen."

"Not hungry."

"New Oma, you must eat or you'll die. Do you need the honey bucket? I can put it at the end of the bed for you."

But she's already nodded off. I'll try again later.

Although I've had little sleep and been assaulted by frightful dreams, this waking nightmare is worse. I fight to compose myself, manage to take Lotty, who's become very quiet, to a scant breakfast in the *heim* kitchen and then to school, even though she's eight, old enough to walk herself. Since I've seen terrible things on the streets and don't want her wandering from school to the *heim* on her own, I'll have to return and fetch her before I go to work. But then she'll be alone with New Oma for the whole night.

I'm becoming frantic. New Oma is too sick to look after Lotty any longer, Lotty too young to look after New Oma, and I have to work or we'll starve. Like Mameh, I want to take the easy way out. Unlike Mameh, I know I can't, though I'm completely overwhelmed, swamped, as though I've been dropped into the East China Sea and it's closing over my head. I have no idea what to do next.

CHAPTER 22

I go to the Green Lily, return early in the morning. I go a second night, turning away as I see Hans through a haze of cigarette smoke. He's dancing with one of the café's Chinese girls. His presence both warms and freezes my heart, but for once I've no time to think about him. I'm too worried about my family.

Walking quickly back to the *heim* early in the morning, I find New Oma asleep and snoring softly, her mouth open. Lotty is watching over her. Scared, Lotty jumps at every snore, every little jerk of New Oma's. I send her to bed and watch over New Oma myself. She has done so much for us, she has shared everything she has and is loving besides, especially to Lotty. I can't bear to think of her dying. There have been too many deaths already. While I'm watching her, I have an idea that might just work. It's worth a try, anyway.

Later in the morning I set out on my quest for Yoshi. I've been hunting all over Shanghai for him since the day our plan to steal from the Japanese bombed, to use an apt expression. At last I remember where I might find him. I guess correctly. He's in the small library behind The Lion bookshop, asleep with his head lying on his folded arms at one of the tables. The table is piled high with books, just as I'd expect. As I call his name he starts, accidentally knocking one of the piles to the floor with his elbow. He drops to his knees to pick up the books.

"Where are you camping out?" I ask him. "Apart from here, I mean."

"Everywhere and nowhere, as I told you. I'm like the coolies, but without a rickshaw."

"Is where you sleep comfortable?"

"What do you think?"

"Shh," hisses the man next to him. "You're supposed to keep quiet in the library. No talking."

We step outside, and I tell Yoshi of the situation at the *heim*. "But early this morning I had an idea. And I was wondering," I say slowly, "how would it be if you lived with us, and stayed with Lotty and New Oma while I work? You'd have a more comfortable place to sleep, and it would put my mind at rest while I do my shift at the café."

"Your neighbours wouldn't like it. An unrelated young woman and young man living in the same space? Oy vey!"

"I'm sure they gossip about me already. I don't care. And in any case, we wouldn't be sleeping together. You could have my cot, and Lotty and I would share. There wouldn't be many days we'd want to use the cot at the same time anyway." I've figured out every detail of what I'm going to say in advance, and gallop through my words. "You could take her to school while I sleep, and I'd collect her and bring her home before work. The nights I'm off, usually Wednesdays, you'd be free to go anywhere you want, and every day you could eat my breakfast in the kitchen. I never feel hungry after work. An added attraction — there's now a bookmobile in front of the Ward Street *heim*." I take a deep breath. Actually it's more like a gasp.

Yoshi looks even thinner than usual, face green tinged, eyes pink and watery, probably from exhaustion, possibly also from our debacle at the Japanese installation. Shock seems to have set in. He's lost all his sparkle and wizardy ways, just stands and stares into the distance with his hands dangling at his sides before looking at his boots. It's as if I'm not there. I'm beginning to fear for him also.

"I'll think about it," is his only reply. No Chinese candies or bubble gum materializes from his sleeves today. No sparklers. He likely has none left.

"Think hard, please. Izo won't come because she's still annoyed with me, and I have no one else to ask. I'm terrified that sooner or later New Oma will die during the night while I'm at work. How awful do you think that would be for Lotty?"

"You're shivering again, Freda." I hear his tongue clicking against the roof of his mouth when he speaks. He's dehydrated, has probably not had any food or drink today. "That officer could have killed us, you know that?"

"I've thought about it a lot. It's perhaps because winter is coming," I reply, "the season of sadness and loss. The number of dead on the streets triples." I don't know why I say this. It's not in the least helpful to either of us.

He doesn't respond. Standing outside The Lion with his eyes still down, Yoshi seems closed and vulnerable. I inwardly weep for him. But interpreting his silence as a no, I turn and walk away slowly, devastated for both of us.

In the afternoon, when I go to fetch Lotty from school, Yoshi is in the schoolyard waiting for her. "I've decided to take you up on your offer, divine Fräulein," he murmurs with his eyes half-closed. "It will be easier on all of us, especially you." He magicks up a candy for my sister. And from then on, we take care of New Oma together, me during the day, constantly interrupting my sleep, and Yoshi at night so I can work. To my despair, even with our assistance and attempts to make her comfortable, New Oma grows ever weaker.

CHAPTER 23

After serving drinks and galumphing around the stage all evening with patrons who have multiple tickets and two left feet, I take a few minutes' break, sitting down at one of the tables at the back of the café as my back is killing me. I'd never do this if the boss were here, but I saw him leave an hour ago. A customer standing behind me reaches over my shoulder to drop a ticket in my lap.

"Ask someone else," I say. "I'm too tired to waltz right now."

"It's you I wish to dance with. Stop hiding from me, Freda." The voice, husky and caressing, resurfaces from the long-ago palimpsest in which I buried its owner. The voice is deeper, smoother, more confident than it used to be. Its German is soft as velvet. But there's no mistaking the timbre of it: it belongs to Hans. My heart flutters against my ribs like a bird trying to escape its cage. I feel so faint I can't respond, don't even have the strength to pick the ticket up to throw back at him.

He walks around the table to face me, clicking his heels together. He's in full Nazi uniform. Suddenly the last days of my life in Berlin, which I've constantly tried to obliterate, rise to the forefront of my mind. Like a secret door in my skull they unlock and open. I once more see Hans on the street, a swaggering recruit of the Hitler Youth. I hear the shots ring out at the Jewish bakery, dead Jews piled like garbage on the road. I see a synagogue burning, hear the people trapped inside screaming. But worst of all, I see the demonic faces of the Nazis who dragged Tateh away.

"Get lost."

"You can't seriously believe I haven't noticed you, Freda," he goes on, as if I've not spoken, as if there has never been any bad feeling between us. "Even though you keep your eyes down or turn away so I can't see your face, I've known it was you since I first came into the Green Lily. I'm so happy you're still alive, but sad to find you working in such a toxic dump. I've come in every night I could since I recognized you. I was just waiting for an opportunity to speak to you. When, that is, your bodyguard wasn't around."

"Bodyguard?"

"The pale boy in the black hat."

"I have no idea what you're talking about."

"Of course you do. He's obviously here to defend your virtue. But it doesn't matter. He's not here now, hasn't been for days. The rules say that if I buy a ticket, I can dance with any girl I want to. I want to dance with you. So that's what I'm going to do."

"I don't want to have anything to do with you," I say, shying away, but he's impossible to resist. He pulls me up and holds me tight, one strong arm pressing into my back, the other imprisoning my hand as we begin to dance. I feel a flush of shame and excitement. Isn't this what I've always wanted — to be with Hans — though I've denied it to myself? The band is playing "I Only Have Eyes for You," and Hans is singing the words softly, to me and me only, in English.

He's crying. "I was only a child when I joined the Hitler Youth, Freda. Maybe eleven or twelve, certainly not more than that. I believed everything I was told. It wasn't until later that I realized how horrifying Hitler was, how evil his policies. I despised myself for not having seen through him from the start, hated my parents for idolizing him, but I had already graduated to the army, so after a lot of soul-searching I decided to use my knowledge and position for the good of others. People like you."

Are those real or crocodile tears? I don't know whether he's telling the truth or lying. He means me to feel sympathetic, I'm sure, but though I have a sneaking desire to do so, I restrain myself. He's a Nazi after all, a Nazi in a Nazi uniform. He might have killed people. He might have committed atrocities. Perhaps he's out to snare me, to kill my little family. I can't trust him, and, trembling, pull an imaginary veil over my face.

"I'll show you how caring and in earnest I am. I'll be here every night I'm not on duty."

"Then I'll stay home."

"Oh, but you can't, my dear. You need the money." There is a hint of triumph in his smile.

Later, he shadows me back to the *heim*, halting behind me when I stop to give my Chinese friend Song some Green Lily leftovers.

"There's a Nazi following you," Song whispers timidly, backing into a deeply shadowed recess.

"Don't worry about him. He won't hurt either of us," I reply, though I'm not at all sure I'm right. But Song has vanished. It's beginning to sleet, stinging ice pellets hitting my face like in my nightmare. Nevertheless I take a very long way home, weaving through a labyrinth of narrow streets and alleys, hiding in doorways, alternately walking and attempting to run. I almost cripple my ankles in my high heels as I slip on the icy roadway and trip over a corpse lying like a log on the pavement.

The dead on the streets don't worry me as much any longer. They're not related to me, and I've seen too many of them to worry or care about them, though the dead babies still sadden me. I scramble away from the corpse and stand up fast, beginning again to slide through the icy mess. I don't want Hans to catch me. I don't want him to see where I live. My pulse thundering in a wild tattoo, I try to shake him off. As I reach home, I believe I've been successful.

But "Good night, Freda," Hans says softly as I reach the corner of Ward Street. "I'll see you tomorrow. Sleep well."

I dash across the road, enter the *heim*, and clang the door shut. As I do so, I believe I hear him call out, "*Heil* Hitler." Perhaps he really does say it, but why would he? To me of all people? My brain, continuing to play tricks on me, even imagines him making the Nazi salute. I try to consign Hans to an imaginary box, cover him with tissue paper as though he's a china doll that can be taken back to the toy store for a refund. But he's not a doll. He's a man, and he resists. He breathes and speaks even now. I'll have to see him again in the Green Lily; I can't conquer his alarming presence in my brain. He's moving in and taking over.

Reaching my family's little corner, I peel off my dress and hang it up on the rail. In the grim dawn light, it looks like a ghostly double of Mameh. My shoes clack to the floor. I rinse my stockings out in a basin and hang them up next to my dress. They resemble a hangman's ropes. I feel as though I've just escaped some ghastly evil, at least for the present, but still suffering from contact with Hans, I splash my face and arms in the cold water of the basin.

After glancing at New Oma to make sure she's still breathing — she is, but only just — I push Lotty over to make space for myself in our shared cot. She murmurs about Mameh, dreaming out loud. I know she's dreaming of her, because she keeps saying, "Never mind, never mind, never mind!" in what sounds like an imitation of Mameh's voice. I huddle under our thin blanket. Despairing, chilled in mind and body, I cuddle up to my sister to take advantage of her warmth. She turns away.

"Ugh, you're icky. Keep your freezing feet to yourself. Give me back some blanket," Lotty mumbles, before again falling asleep and snoring like a steam engine. She's had a cold for days, like many of the refugees. Sickness spreads faster than a rumour in the *heim*. Yoshi, wide awake, his face drawn and ashen in the shadows, has been watching me from the moment I entered our cubicle. He looks like a sorcerer's owl with his big, unblinking eyes. It's as if he understands what's happening to me. As if he *knows*. But he says nothing.

"I saw you last night with that Nazi," Izo says, accosting me on the street as I go to work. "I couldn't sleep and was looking out the window. What's up?"

"Nothing," I say. "Keep your mouth shut and your jaw locked."

"Nothing begets something. Or is it nothing? From a play called *King Lear*," Izo says with pride. She must have learned the words from Yoshi, the Shakespeare expert who spouts quotes suitable for every occasion. She couldn't have studied *King Lear* herself. She's not bright enough. Perhaps she and Yoshi see each other while I'm otherwise employed. I'm not going to worry about it right now. I have far more important matters to cope with.

CHAPTER 24

When I arrive at work the next evening, Hans is sitting with his band of friends, all of them singing raucous Nazi songs and toasting one another with large flagons of beer. Chinese and British customers look at them with disdain. The Nazis even out-noise the Japanese, who are also drunk. As soon as Hans sees me he quits his comrades and comes over, pulling out a chair for me and ordering costly wine with a meal, which he lays before me as if I'm an honoured guest. Is he drunk too? Is that why he's being so generous?

"I'll eat the rest later," I say after a few mouthfuls. I want to save what's left for my family. The boss leaves us alone for the most part, although he asks, late in the evening, if we'd like to go upstairs together. I wince. He's made a bad mistake.

"Can't you see that this is a lady?" Hans shouts, his birthmark burning red. He removes his gun from its holster and clatters it onto the table. I recoil in horror.

So does the boss. As customers begin to scramble for the door and the other Nazis cheer Hans's bravado, my employer bows and scrapes like a coolie, all the while keeping his eye on the pistol. "Apologies, *mein 'err*. I made a terrible error. No insult intended." He's not anxious to tangle with the tall, well-built German. It could well be his last tangle, especially if the German's Nazi friends join the fray. But Hans can also be a very generous tipper, and if there's anything the boss really lusts after, it's money. He's not about to kill the goose-stepper that lays the golden egg. Hans dismisses him with a wave of his hand.

"Shall we dance, Freda? The band has just begun to play a favourite song of mine. I must get you a new dress. You wear the same outfit every night, and it's getting quite ragged."

"I'll take care of it myself," I say. But of course, I can't.

"Be careful of him," whispers Leila when Hans has left. She's one of the other girls who work at the café.

"Careful how?"

She shrugs her shoulders. "Just careful, that's all. They're all a bunch of liars." Does she mean men in general or Nazis in particular? Leila's a Jewish refugee, like I am, so she's likely speaking of the Nazis.

"Yes, you're right. I'll be sure to be careful." But there's been something devilish in me since I met Hans again, so it's possible I won't be.

Meanwhile, a buzz goes around the café in half a dozen different languages: The Japanese are rounding up the English and French, and any Americans they can find. Many of the Japanese soldiers pay their bills in a hurry, throwing coins down on tables, quitting the café. The Nazis leave their drinks unfinished in their haste to clear out. A drunken Englishman stops by their table to finish the dregs of their beer. The boss is practically crying at the loss of revenue. "What does this mean?" I ask Leila.

"It means things are going to get even worse," she says. "Just you wait and see."

CHAPTER 25

One evening follows another in lockstep. As the nights pass I become accustomed, in return for kisses, to being gifted with expensive clothing, jewellery and furs, decadent meals at expensive restaurants in the French Concession, fine wines and pastries. I love the attention. And there's no possibility of being found out by Yoshi, who would be furious, telling me I'm fraternizing with the enemy, as I suppose I am. Yoshi's job is to look after New Oma while I'm out, and to all appearances he takes it seriously. So I'm not likely to see him at the Green Lily or in the Concession any time soon.

Hans hasn't yet been given his marching orders. He whispers that he belongs to the remnants of The White Rose, an organization dedicated to killing Hitler. He warns me not to tell anyone, or he will be guillotined. Most members of The White Rose — some university students — have already been executed using this brutish method, he murmurs in my ear as we dance. The White Rose organization is all but stamped out, but he hopes to re-energize it. Either that, or join another anti-Hitler organization.

I'm honoured that he confides in me, but the word *guillotine* cuts like a knife. For a moment I can't breathe. I can't stand the thought of Hans being executed. I do want to believe that he really plans to kill Hitler. I also want to believe that even if he does get close enough to kill the Führer, he won't be harmed. I want more than anything in the world to trust him. When I see his face so cold and obdurate when he speaks of Hitler, I'm sure I can.

He's extremely generous, and that pits me against my better self. When he holds his hand out, full of silver *Reichsmark*, I let him drop the coins one by one into my palm. "We are playing the cash game," he smiles. I continue to participate even though the swastikas on the backs of the coins disgust me, convincing myself that I'm acting charitably, that this treasure trove will feed my little family for weeks.

Light as autumn leaves, paper bills tossed up by him drift down for me to gather. Although I demurred at first, wouldn't accept what he offered, after a while I couldn't help but be charmed. Hans the man is so different from Yoshi the boy. Hans is serious, Yoshi a joker. Hans is my protector, Yoshi my sidekick. Hans, with money to spare, conjures up silver cash. Yoshi, penniless, waves sparklers in the air and finds stolen candies behind my ear. I shouldn't compare Hans with Yoshi, but I can't stop myself. The contrasts are too obvious to miss. As time goes on, Hans races past Yoshi to take first place in the Shanghai heart stakes.

Hans was my best friend many years ago; I desperately want him to be my best friend again. If he were interested in a closer relationship, he could mean even more to me. I persuade myself without much trouble that we were parted by circumstance, not hatred.

Waving the white flag of surrender, conveniently forgetting the more dubious aspects of his personality, I lock his gun away in my mind's vault, along with the hateful Nazi songs he sings with his fellows, his occasional viciousness toward those who cross him, his need for control. I tell myself that these faults are really subterfuge, so that he can, while pretending to be a Nazi, work against Hitler without being detected. I also tell myself again that I'm only continuing to see him for the sake of Lotty, New Oma, Song and Yoshi, who all need my help. But of course, it's not that simple. Neither is it true.

However, whether Hans is trustworthy or not, by accepting his money I'm beholden to him. But more important at the moment than this debt, and how or when it might be called in, is the fact that I can feed and clothe my family. My being obligated to Hans in return for my family's health strikes me as a more than fair exchange. They won't starve like some of the other refugees. Almost everyone still living at the *heim* is in desperate straits, now down to one bowl of watery soup per person per day as charitable Jewish funds run out.

But not knowing when all of Hans's largesse might end, I still make sure to go to work at the Green Lily Café six nights a week as usual, stowing my excess wages under my bed as Mameh used to. Soon I will be able to go out house hunting, find my family a small apartment in the International Settlement, where the air and the streets are cleaner and I'm less likely to find a rat under my bed, bedbugs in my nightdress, or spiders weaving webs in my hair. If we should run short of cash when Hans leaves, as he must do sooner or later, I will need to sell the fabulous jewellery, the dresses and furs, to wealthier refugees who live away from the *heim*, though I won't want to. The truth is that the costly and opulent gifts have begun to excite me, just as they did Mameh. I'm ashamed of myself. I remember swearing I'd never be like her, but when I murmur the words costly, *fabulous*, and *opulent* to myself, they roll over my tongue like sweet wine. And these gifts are souvenirs, precious reminders of Hans.

Nevertheless, the proceeds from his gifts — if I can bring myself to part with them — will keep Yoshi, Lotty, and me comfortable for several years. I can help Song out too. I will be able to afford a private doctor for New Oma. But for the moment I keep everything Hans has given me in a locked cupboard at the Green Lily, changing my clothes when I arrive at work. I tell the boss I need the cupboard to keep my evening wear in good condition as the winter grows ever more ferocious, as Shanghai is slammed by driving winds and torrential rain and occasional snow. Though it's not even December.

"I'm always surprised by winter's savagery; need," I continue, "to buy a pair of galoshes and a raincoat to come and go in."

Although he doesn't appear to be listening, the boss nods. These days he always nods. After his run-in with Hans, he's become spineless as an amoeba when dealing with me. The balance of power has shifted. I'm pretty sure he'll let me do anything I want to; I'm relieved he's not barking at me or threatening me any longer.

It's vital that my cache of treasure remains hidden. A cupboard with a door that locks is, I hope, as secure as the German mint. And it has to be. I don't want Yoshi to find out right now what I have and where I got it. It will cause the most frightful row.

CHAPTER 26

I'm sitting with Hans at the Green Lily, holding hands with him under the table, when a Chinese businessman approaches and asks me very politely if I'd like to dance. Hans doesn't speak Mandarin, but he gets the gist. In a split second he is out of his chair and yelling in German at the businessman, who is new to the Green Lily and has no idea what, if anything, he's done wrong. His hands are trembling. "Sorry, sorry, sir," he says, bowing. "I didn't know she was your property."

I translate for Hans, furious at being thought his property, but he laughs uproariously as he waves the businessman away. "Come on, Freda, let's show that Chink what a real dance looks like." I wince at the word *Chink*, but he's pulling at my hand and I feel that unless I want a quarrel, I have no choice but to take the floor with him. The band is playing a slow and romantic waltz. I lay my head on Hans's shoulder as we dance, and he murmurs, "We could, you know."

"Could what?"

"Live together. I've always adored you. I'll hide you in a flat in the Concession and stay there when I'm off-duty."

"I can't. I have my family to think of. And I wouldn't live with any man — not even you — before marriage."

"Please," he entreats softly. "I'll marry you after the war, I promise. To do so now would be suicide, not only for myself, but for you. I'm supposed to be killing Jews, remember, not marrying one of them."

I gasp at his words. My throat squeezes shut. Before I can recover enough to answer, the door crashes open and Yoshi strides in. Everyone turns to see who the odd, strangely dressed youth is, while he takes in my blue silk dress, jewels, and obvious intimacy with Hans in one long, anguished glance. But he doesn't remark on what he sees. Instead he simply takes hold of my arm, saying, "Freda, you must come home at once. Your oma has died."

"No," I shriek. "She can't have."

"She has," Yoshi says quietly. "Go fetch your coat."

"What's the point of your going if she's already dead? It'll only upset you," Hans says.

"I'm upset already." I fetch my coat from the back of the café. Hans says nothing more, but Yoshi, alert to my pain, puts his arm around me as we leave.

"I'm so sorry, Yoshi — about Hans, that is."

"I already knew. I've known for weeks." His face is wistful. "You tread on my dreams."

I've hurt him badly; I see that now. I didn't realize how much he cared for me. And I don't know how to fix him, get the old magical Yoshi back. Instead I say, "How sad, but what a lovely image that is. Did you make it up?"

"No, though I wish I did. Here's a bit more:"

But I, being poor, have only my dreams;

I have spread my dreams under your feet;
Tread softly because you tread on my dreams.

"Shakespeare?"

"No, Yeats. He expresses how I feel better than I can."

"Oh," I murmur, contrite. "I will try not to tread on your dreams any longer, Yoshi."

"You won't mean to, I know, but you probably will," he says, as we enter the *heim*.

CHAPTER 27

The day after New Oma is buried, I return to the Green Lily, still grieving but in fear of losing my job. It's my day off, but I've come in to make up for some of the time I've missed.

As I enter the café, hoping to see and talk to Hans, he is on his way upstairs with Opal, a pretty Chinese girl who works at the bar. She's wearing a long, lacy dress that I've never seen before, and a ruby tiara, as if she's a princess dressed for the ball. Somehow, despite all her finery, she looks tawdry, and it's a wake-up call for me. Did I look like her — like a prostitute, if I'm honest with myself — when I wore Hans's gifts? Hans, who is shepherding her up the stairs, his hand locked in hers, turns at the sound of my cry. "Hans," I wail. He opens his mouth, as if about to say something, but changes his mind. And after all, what can there be to say? Clearly not expecting me, guilt etched over the faint lines of his face, he raises his free hand in a gesture of defeat. Turning back to Opal, he continues to climb with her to the private rooms on the second floor. His steps are those of an old, beaten man.

What can he be thinking? He knows everything must be

over between us. I try to justify his behaviour by telling myself he's only sleeping with Opal as I won't do the same. It doesn't help.

"See, what did I tell you?" says Leila. "You're gone for a few days and he's already in another woman's bed."

I'm shaking but manage to clarify my position. "He never was in my bed, thank heavens, nor I in his. I thought he would wait till I was ready, but clearly that's not the case." I'm beginning to sob. Tears leak from my eyes.

"Don't cry. You've had a lucky escape. But he was luring you, that was plain to see, into doing what Opal does. Then he'd cast you off like an old glove. I've seen it all before. First come the gifts, then the words of love, then ... well, you know the rest. I was caught by it myself once, but vowed never to be caught again. I hope your turning up gives him a really bad shock, and a pain somewhere unmentionable. He deserves it. The only good Nazi is a dead Nazi," she finishes venomously, a spray of spit accompanying her words.

"You should have told me."

"I tried often enough. You weren't listening. He might act like the most charming man in the world, but he's just a snake. Still, it never does any good telling someone something she'd rather not hear. I guess you had to discover his Nazi fangs for yourself, and were lucky enough to do so before he dug them in deep and ruined your life, before he poisoned you."

Leila, unfortunately, is right. A snake is a snake, after all. Even if it sloughs off its skin, it's the same underneath. I could kick myself for my stupidity. I'm horribly depressed, feel, as well as wretched, desperately ashamed. For days I'm terrified of seeing Hans when I go to work. I feel guilty, as if it was I who behaved badly, not him. But he never appears, although every time I go to sleep he enters through the portal of my dreams;

or, to be more precise, my nightmares. I wake with my teeth clenched and hands shaking. More than once I've bitten my lip or tongue; on awakening I see bright circlets of blood, their design on my pillow reminiscent of Opal's fake ruby tiara. It takes me months to realize that I wasn't really in love with Hans. I loved what I hoped, what I wished him to be. He wore the swastika, symbol of all I hate and despise. How could I have ever have ignored that? Now, since I can't trust him, I'm left with only one question that could exonerate him: Did he really belong to The White Rose organization? I think not. I go back to wearing my old dress to work. Christians would call it a penance. Jews call it *teshuvah*. The boss says it's disgraceful. How can I get customers looking like a country wife?

After months of grieving, with a sudden explosion of energy, I pull all Hans' gifts from the cupboard in the café, arranging them on a blanket in Kungping Road where refugees and others in Hongkew and the settlement come to buy. I attract quite a crowd as I sell my goods, which are mostly flashy and expensive, and so available only to the wealthy. I barter with prospective buyers loudly, anxious to show I'm in earnest. I need to wash my hands of every bit of the finery that's been tainted by Hans. I can't bear to look at it.

I sell Lotty's outgrown clothes too, and New Oma's belongings, keeping only New Oma's brooch with its dangling silver stars to give my sister on her birthday, as well as some of Hans' cash to buy Song a rickshaw so he can earn a living. I'm not sure what to do with the rest of the proceeds. In the end I decide to keep half under the mattress, the way Mameh did. The rest will go straight into the bank. I begin to look for an apartment for Yoshi, Lotty, Song and myself, while giving the cupboard key and my notice to quit to the boss of the Green Lily Café. He's probably delighted to get rid of me.

CHAPTER 28

The Japanese are on every street, in almost every municipal building, in every house and *heim*, demonstrating their control of Shanghai. They are taking over the government of the French Concession and the International Settlement, Yoshi tells me, as well as tightening the reins in Hongkew. The Nazis are very visible too. Hitler wants the Jews of Shanghai to be sent east, a euphemism that we all understand, though it would be west from here. It means the Nazis want us all dispatched to concentration camps, as the Japanese don't seem inclined to imprison us in Shanghai. Word is leaking out that the concentration camps are nothing more than killing grounds. I can't believe it, but Yoshi and Izo — who is back on the scene, apparently having forgiven me — both tell me I'm in denial.

However, in the absence of anything concrete, and the fact that there's nowhere else that we know of willing to accept Jews, the wheels of life continue to turn creakily: Lotty goes to school, unaware of the rumours but still grieving over the loss of New Oma; Song runs his business, pulling the splendid rickshaw I bought him, mainly serving Japanese officers and wealthy Sephardic Jews; Yoshi has decided to help him, so that they each take a shift while the other rests. They work day and night to make a bundle of cash. They refuse to take any more money from me, and in fact insist in giving some of their takings back to me and Lotty. It goes straight into the bank or under my mattress.

With their first quarter's profit they've bought themselves matching brightly coloured Chinese outfits that appeal to Yoshi. He also chooses towering black hats that resemble industrial chimneys for Song and himself. He still loves to dress in exotic if somewhat bizarre costumes, and Song, who idolizes him, is thrilled to be outfitted in the same manner.

Yoshi performs magic tricks for many of the customers; they love to see a few minutes of entertainment after their rickshaw ride and tip him well. "I'm all the rage," he announces proudly, as he produces a bar of banana toffee from under his hat and presents it to me. He knows how I love Palm's banana toffee, occasionally available in the British shops of the International Settlement.

"Don't break your teeth on it," he remarks with a grin.

Yoshi's been building muscles by pulling the rickshaw, but one day he fell while transporting a passenger. The passenger, a doctor, examined him and suggested he was probably anemic. The doctor further suggested that Yoshi eat red meat and liver on a regular basis. Now Yoshi buys it ready-cooked at the market, and makes sure to feed the rest of us with slivers of meat so we don't fall victim to the same disease.

"Ugh, liver," Lotty complains. "I want pickled herring."

"Get it down you," growls Yoshi, "and I'll give you an almond cookie."

He seems curiously untouched by the fact that we soon may all be carted away and liquidated. For the most part, Yoshi lives his life in the now, and his frequent highs and lows often have little to do with what's happening in the world. Perhaps that's for the best.

Only I have nothing to do, and sitting on my cot in the *heim* all day is, to put it bluntly, a torment as well as a waste of time. I thought I'd enjoy doing nothing for a while, just spending the days lazing around in bed and the park nearby. I sometimes take Lotty to the park too, but it's not a good idea to go in winter as it's freezing outside. So instead, I sit in the *heim*, each hour stretching to eternity. I try to knit Lotty a scarf, but I'm allergic to the wool and my hands break out in blisters. I attempt to read, but, unlike Yoshi, I'm not much of a reader lately, because huge negative thoughts worm their way out of my brain and slither around the text. Perhaps I need glasses. But in the meantime, I have nothing to do but agonize over our precarious situation.

I'm terrified that Hans and Co. might be preparing to round us up. The British, French, and American soldiers in Shanghai are already being interred in Japanese prison camps. I've heard that some of the Americans were decapitated. It made me throw up in the honey bucket.

The violent attacks of the Japanese on the British and their allies in Shanghai and elsewhere have terrorized me, as I'm anticipating even worse treatment; and I'm wondering whether Tateh could possibly still be alive. Do the concentration camps really only exist to kill Jews and others the Nazis consider undesirable? Will they cart us away as they did Tateh, or at least try to get the Japanese to do so? How can human beings be so devastatingly cruel to one another? I feel as though I'm standing on a pile of dry logs and tinder that Hans or his cronies are about to set fire to. Dear God, I don't want to be burned or gassed for the non-existent crime of being Jewish. Please don't abandon me and my family.

I have to find something to occupy my mind so that I don't keep panicking about what the future might hold, so that I don't keep inventing scenarios till I go completely crazy. I start to prowl the streets and alleys as I used to, trying to find a job, preferably part-time, so I can spend the afternoons with Lotty. She needs me to hang onto now that New Oma's gone. How confusing life must be for her, raised first by Mameh and Tateh, then New Oma, then me in my ineffectual way. I don't think she even remembers what Tateh looked like. I hardly do myself.

I'm not good with kids, but I hug her, kiss her, and take her to the market for treats, the way New Oma did. But I can't find part-time work. It's hard to find any work at all. Most employment advertisements in local papers, on billboards and shop doors read, "Refugees need not apply."

Although out of Germany, I still feel the chill wind of discrimination. I draw my coat tighter around me and belt it securely. The days are cold. The shopkeepers colder. Although I'm well-dressed and well-spoken — at least in my own opinion — they smell me out, like dogs hunting a fox. And like me, they must feel that the Japanese are watching them. They're afraid to put a foot wrong, especially by hiring a Jewish refugee now the Japanese are officially in league with the Nazis. Indeed, with the economy so bad, there's very little hiring going on at all. Instead, many employees are being dismissed.

Finding an apartment is just as difficult. Who, after all, would want to rent to two young German refugees, a failed *yeshiva* boy, and a Chinese urchin? In the end I resort to telling landlords lies.

"The young man and I are married." Lie! "My sister lives with us as our mother is dead." Lie! "The Chinese boy is our servant." Lie! "We also have," I say with my fingers crossed behind my back, "a surfeit of money from a business acquisition." Lie! Lie! Lie! Of course I mean the selling of old clothes and the money the rickshaw brings in, but how are they to know that? My description deceives them into thinking we manage a great enterprise. Nobody questions why we're trying to find a flat the size of a burial plot when we're so wealthy.

Within a month of starting my search, I find a suitable apartment in the International Settlement, just a room really, with a sink and running water. But it feels like a palace after the *heim*. A Chinese boy goes from house to house along the street each morning, I'm told, emptying honey buckets for a few pennies, and there's a small patch of green in the back, which Lotty will love to play in. We might even be allowed by the landlord to grow some vegetables.

"I hope there's a Chinese candy tree in the garden," Yoshi says to Lotty. "Just think, you could pick all your favourite flavours and pop them in your mouth, just like this one." He produces an orange sweet from behind her ear with a flourish. "Or you could make a candy pie with them."

"Do candies really grow on trees?" she asks in wonderment.

"Indubitably," Yoshi replies, winking at me.

"I like the purple ones best," she says.

"There'll be plenty of those, you can be sure of that. Purple candy trees grow like weeds in Shanghai."

We start to pack our paltry possessions. We can't lug the cots out of the *heim*, of course, at least not without being noticed, so we'll have to sleep on the floor at first. But we spirit away blankets and sheets, tin cups and plates and cutlery. Song takes some of our belongings in the rickshaw to our new address. We mean to follow him. But just as we're about to move out of the *heim*, we're shoved back in.

"No leaving, no leaving," shouts a fat Japanese officer with black and gold teeth when he sees our clumsy packages, our armfuls of clothing.

"Let us pass," demands Yoshi. "We have lodgings somewhere else."

"Where you go?"

"To the International Settlement."

"No can go. Get back in big house."

"On whose authority are we to stay here?" asks Yoshi.

The officer raises his pistol and shoves it against Yoshi's stomach. Lotty drops her package and hurtles back inside. Yoshi holds his ground. "That's pretty good authority," he says, smiling, though I can see his hands are trembling. Petrified, I stand beside him. How can I abandon him now to chase after my sister as if we're playing tag?

"Have a candy," Yoshi says in a friendly fashion, as he stands welcoming disaster. "Want to see a card trick?"

"No zank much you," replies the officer, clearly baffled by Yoshi's behaviour. This isn't, after all, the way things are supposed to go.

"On whose authority, really?" asks Yoshi.

"High up Japanese army man. Says all Jews to live area Hongkew." The officer waves his gun at a new sign on the *heim* wall. Asking for permission to look at it, which he grants, I run over and read the notice aloud:

DESIGNATED AREA FOR STATELESS REFUGEES
BECAUSE OF MILITARY NECESSITY, THE RESIDENTIAL AND BUSINESS AREAS OF STATELESS REFUGEES IN THE SHANGHAI AREA WILL BE RESTRICTED TO AN AREA WITHIN THE INTERNATIONAL SETTLEMENT EAST OF THE LINE CONNECTING CHOHORO, MOKAIRO AND TODOTSUDO, CHAOUFONG ROAD, MUIRHEAD ROAD AND DENT ROAD.

I scan the rest quickly. "Yoshi, we're all being herded into a tiny area of Hongkew. A *ghetto*." I stumble over the hateful word, and we both quail. Yoshi looks panic-stricken. The Nazis forced his family into a Polish ghetto before they disappeared. The last we heard was that they and many others were transported to Treblinka after an uprising. It appears that the Nazis are cleaning out all the Jewish ghettos, sending the inhabitants "east." They've asked their pals the Japanese — so far unsuccessfully — to do the same thing with those of us in Shanghai. But this could be the Japanese's first step.

"Zank much you. We go inside now play *igo*, game of life death," says Yoshi, still shaking but not missing the opportunity to mimic the Japanese, as well as issue a mild threat. He almost always feels the need to assert himself against authority — as he did in the *yeshiva* — or ridicule it. He constantly stands on the edge of a precipice as if waiting for someone to fling him over.

Luckily the officer doesn't notice Yoshi's mocking impersonation of him. His English isn't nearly good enough to realize that he's being caricatured. He lowers his gun and bows. We kowtow to him, banging our heads on the ground, and he goes away. We smirk at his absurd walk. Wider than he is tall, with skinny legs, he looks like a disgruntled chicken as he picks his way through the smelly garbage of Ward Street.

"I can't figure out how his legs hold the rest of his body up," Yoshi says. Laughing, he grabs my hand and starts to dance a hora with me. Lotty, creeping back to see if the coast is clear, joins in.

CHAPTER 29

never thought I'd be pleased to be back in the *heim*; but now, with thousands of Jews pouring into the one square mile designated for us in Hongkew, and with the Chinese, although free to leave our ghetto, for the most part staying put as they have nowhere else to go, I count myself lucky we have somewhere to live. And we each have a bed to ourselves too, in our old corner. It's just as well, as I'd forgotten to grab our money from under the mattress when we were trying to move out.

Lotty's cot is up against the wall, and I'm in the middle. Yoshi sleeps closest to the curtain.

"We're the three bears," Lotty calls out one night, delighted. "I'm the baby bear, you're mameh bear, Freda, and Yoshi is great big tateh bear. I wonder where we can find a Goldilocks."

"Don't even think about it," I reply. "We're as crowded as matches in a matchbox as it is."

"Spoilsport," she sniffs. It's become one of her favourite words. She's never grown out of using it, but on the other hand, she's never grown into using the more colourful descriptions I hear on the streets. Lotty often surprises me. She's now only a couple of years younger than I was when we left Berlin, but seems a good deal more childish than I was at eight. She still sucks her thumb when she's tired, and frequently uses what I call toddler talk. It drives me crazy. Perhaps New Oma coddled her too much. Or maybe she feels safer in this scary atmosphere if she takes refuge in babyhood.

"Growl, Yoshi, growl, you soppy tateh bear!"

"Sorry, Lotty, I'm asleep," Yoshi, says, yawning.

"How can you be asleep when you're talking to me, silly?"

"Leave him be, Lotty."

The poor boy must be exhausted. He's on daytime shift with the rickshaw, trundling it up and down our small Hongkew area all day, confined as we are to the ghetto. He tried to get an exemption so he could go further afield, but was refused. He was the first, with scores more to follow. There aren't many who can afford him here in Hongkew. Song, because he's Chinese, is not restricted, so he takes the rickshaw around the rest of Shanghai at night, hoping for customers. They have become few and far between, are now limited mostly to Nazi or Japanese military, which I know scares him. He tries to return the rickshaw early each morning to Yoshi, but sometimes he ends up across the city delivering a customer, so it takes time for him to come back. He arrives at the *heim* looking half dead. I told him he's more that welcome to sleep in Yoshi's bed during the day, but he prefers to sleep on the road, sitting up with his back against the *heim* wall.

"So I can go quickly to Yoshi if he needs me," he says simply. This seems unlikely, nonsensical really. How would he know if Yoshi needs him? Wouldn't it be just as easy to reach Yoshi from the *heim* as from the street, if by any miracle he does, within earshot, call for help? It's more likely that Song can't remember sleeping anywhere but in an alley, so in an odd but understandable way he finds it familiar and comforting.

It's a common enough sight in Shanghai, young coolies sleeping on the street. But it's also a common sight to see them dead of starvation or cold in some shadowed alleyway, before their tattered remains are swept away and burned or buried. I know I can't do anything for the others, can't take on the cares of everyone, but I just can't stand the thought of such a calamity happening to Song. Though he must be horribly cold in winter, when the rickshaw is there during the day, because Yoshi is too shattered to take it out, Song sleeps under it so, as he says, he can guard it from thieves. I can't get him to come in, even when I promise him a new rickshaw to replace the old if it's stolen from him or Yoshi. "No, Mistress Freda," he replies in Wu, "it is all I have ever owned. It is important to me. No other rickshaw would do. I have grown as fond of it as I would a favourite pet. I cannot stand the thought of losing it."

One cold afternoon it begins to rain as Yoshi comes running back to the *heim*, dragging the rickshaw behind him. "Come quickly," he calls to me, his lips as white as the rest of his face. "You have to see this." He abandons the rickshaw to Song and rushes me to the edge of the ghetto. We take a few more steps forward, as at the moment only an imaginary line in our square mile of Hongkew encloses us, not barriers. It's raining heavily now, icy water splashing up from the ground, forming rivulets that run along the centre of the street.

"Get away from here," says a severe-looking Japanese soldier, "or I arrest you, put you in truck too."

We comply quickly. But not before I gasp at what I see in front of me. It's a staging area. Many of the remaining residents of the International Settlement and the French Concession — left behind when the Jews were pushed into the ghetto — are being loaded into Japanese army trucks. They're all sodden.

Some are half-dressed. Most, caught off guard, have only the clothes or pajamas they stand up in. If they had luggage, much of it has been left behind. People are crushed as the Japanese force more and more of them into the open trucks. There's no attempt to keep families together. Babies are screaming, frightened husbands and wives trying in vain to hang on to each other and their children as they're loaded like freight into different vehicles and driven away.

"Dear God," I say. "What can be happening? They're not Jews, so why are they being treated this way?" I can't bear to look at them, at their dismayed expressions, their despair.

"But the Japanese are at war, Freda. They're battling our allies: the British, Americans ..."

"I know all that, but these people are *civilians*. The Japanese aren't supposed to cart them away to who knows where."

"The Nazis weren't supposed to send the Jews east, either, but it hasn't stopped them." Defying the Japanese soldier's order, Yoshi darts into the road to rescue a baby who's fallen from a truck before it's run over.

He's risking his life. Only two days ago I saw an old Jewish man, deep in his prayer book, beheaded in the street for neglecting to bow to a Japanese officer who was walking by. *Flash* went the officer's sword as it caught the sun on the way down. Everything happened so fast that for a moment I thought I'd imagined it. But the old man's bloody remains bore witness to his death, the torn pages of his Torah floating away like confetti, his severed head rolling across the ground like a soccer ball.

My legs were too weak to carry me from the scene. I crouched in a doorway for hours, too numb to cry. To my shame I soiled my pants. But even if Yoshi had been standing beside me, even if he'd seen the whole shocking episode culminating in the old man's death, which demonstrated what the Japanese were capable of, it would have made no difference. He would still be standing in the middle of the road today with a baby in his arms. He would still be just as daring. That's who he is. My best friend, Yoshi — who acts with fearful bravery.

"He's mine. Give him to me," a woman shrieks. Yoshi climbs onto one of the truck wheels and hands him over. "You're an angel," the woman says, tears mixed with rain rolling down her face. The baby is bleeding from the fall, his face waxy. I pray he'll survive.

There is sudden quiet. The trucks have gone. The soldiers have vanished. It's as if they were never there, had never scooped up all those civilians. Although I'm with Yoshi, I feel isolated and alone, as if I'm the last person left in Shanghai. "Yoshi, Yoshi," I sob, "if the Japanese are removing all those people who've never harmed a soul, what will they do to *us*?"

"The world has gone mad," he says, shaking his head. He has no solution to offer me.

1944

The Year of the Monkey

CHAPTER 30

We are not hauled away. In fact, I found out from Yoshi, who seems to know everything before anyone else does, that Hitler had sent engineers over to build gas chambers in which to suffocate us, as well as ovens in which to incinerate our corpses, but the Japanese refused to cooperate. I'm both scared and thankful, try to keep as many of the horrific stories as possible away from Lotty. She doesn't need to hear them.

Although we're still in the ghetto and not a death camp, our lives, restricted as they are, begin to change for the worse. The roads are crowded from one end to the other. The *heims* are crammed with Jews who have nowhere else to go. The banks begin to hold back Jewish money that's been paid in, not allowing clients to access their accounts. Thank God there is still cash under my mattress.

Barriers are set up. Long lineups of people stand at the checkpoint, trying to obtain special passes so that they can get to their jobs outside the ghetto. Some are given passes, some not, at the whim of a small but aggressive man known as Mr. Goya, the Japanese man in charge. People who stand for hours or even days in the line only to be denied exit IDs say that Goya screamed at them for no reason while jumping on top of his desk. He's crazy, drunk with power and seething with anger. I'm told this by a man in our *heim* denied a pass to go to his job, which is only two streets away from the ghetto.

I'm still hunting for work, more seriously now that half our money is unavailable to us, and today, walking along the crowded street on my way to fetch Lotty from school, I see a sign on a shop window:

THE BELL CHIME

LADIES AND GENTLEMEN, WE CAN MEND YOUR BROKEN CLOCKS AND WATCHES.

WE ALSO SELL NEW MERCHANDISE FOR THOSE OF REFINED TASTE.

HELPFUL STAFF. REASONABLE RATES.

PLEASE FEEL FREE TO ENTER AND VIEW OUR NEW PREMISES.

A smaller sign to the side of the door reads: *Help wanted. Refugees knowledgeable about timepieces welcome to apply.*

Not entirely sure that what I've read is true, I step inside. Clocks are ticking loudly. The proprietor greets me with a huge smile. "You look familiar," he says.

"It's me, Freda, Herr Rubin. I came into your other store long ago to ask for a job."

"Are you still looking? My assistant was a Gentile so wasn't pushed into the ghetto like I was. Goodness knows what's happened to him since. So many rumours, so much tragedy."

"So much tragedy indeed." I wait, my breath stopped in my throat, for him to continue.

"I rented this shop from a Chinese family who were moving away. I've been searching for assistance from someone with a knowledge of the business. Dozens are clamouring for a job, but they just don't have that passion for clocks that you and I have." He returns his spectacles, which are in danger of falling off, back to the bridge of his nose. His hair has turned completely white. "To be honest, there aren't many of us about. In any case, if you're interested, you would fit the bill perfectly. I would have gotten in touch, *maidel,* but I lost your address. And now you're so grown-up I hardly recognize you. And you've cut off your beautiful braids."

"I *am* still looking for employment, and nothing would please me more than to work for you," I reply, restraining myself from jumping up and down.

"Wonderful! Serendipity!" He nods and nods again, catching his *kipa* as it falls off his head. He fastens it back on with a hairpin, reminding me of the long-ago doctor at the hospital. "But I can only employ you part-time, I'm afraid."

"That's exactly what I'm looking for. I can't believe you really have a job for me. "

We shake hands and grin at each other. He tells me I can start as soon as I like.

"Thank you, thank you, Herr Rubin," I say. "You don't know how much this means to me and my family. I'll start tomorrow morning, if that's all right."

"It will be more than all right. It will be marvellous. We will get on very well, you and I, Freda. I'm sure of it. I am only sorry I couldn't hire you when you first came in."

As I walk to the door, at least a hundred clocks chime, cuckoo, and ring the half hour. I'm reminded of Tateh, and always will be, I'm sure, at The Bell Chime. I yearn to hear his voice. Could he still be alive? The question haunts me. I miss him terribly, so stand still and take a minute to listen to the clocks chiming. Not daring to wait longer, I try to put thoughts of Tateh aside and start to run. I need to collect Lotty before she takes it into her head to walk home on her own or, worse, go exploring.

As I rush toward Lotty's school, I realize how kind Herr Rubin is being to me, and once again rejoice. I'm ecstatic about my new job; it's so different from working at the Green Lily Café. Damn the bank for confiscating my funds. But now, thanks to The Bell Chime, I have the wherewithal for us to live comfortably without the cash imprisoned in its vaults.

Who would ever have guessed I'd have the luck to meet up with Herr Rubin again? Certainly not me. Yoshi sometimes calls me Fräulein Gloom and Doom. I often, he says, see only the worst in any situation.

"It's not easy to see anything good," I counter, "with people starving, having their heads cut off or dying in gas chambers." But this is a red-letter day. It's like celebrating Chanukah the way we did when I was young, replete with *latkes, gelt, dreidels,* and candles burning brightly on the windowsill. It's not nearly as good as having Tateh back with us again, but if the streets and alleys were less congested, I'd still turn handsprings, as Yoshi does, all the way to my sister's school.

CHAPTER 31

*A*n alarm goes off. I crawl to the end of my bunk and dress for work — not casually for my day at The Bell Chime, but more suggestively for the Green Lily Café. Donning the long dress, silk stockings, and high heels requisite to my job, I look at my reflection in my shard of a mirror so I can apply makeup. I start with mascara. But after a moment or two I realize it's not me I see reflected in the mirror, it's Mameh. She and I are wearing identical outfits and both have golden glitter in our hair. Like me, she's putting on heavy maquillage. As I apply dark red lipstick and powder to my face, she paints her lips the colour of blood and puffs white powder onto her cheeks. Her powder turns into a gelatinous mess.

"Get lost, Mameh!" I yell, shutting my eyes. But when I peek at the glass again she's still standing there. I put my hand on the mirror to brush her away. She does the same thing, our fingers touching. She tries to hold onto my hand. I break away from hers.

"I always knew you'd become me, Freda," she screams. I notice black gaps in her teeth when she opens her lips; snakes slither out of her mouth. Jumping through the mirror she begins to chase me, her fingernails turning into sharp talons and her face evil. The heim *is changing into a cave, macabre and eerie. Gore drips down walls. Spiders, enormous enough to catch rats, cast webs with filaments thick as ropes. Headless men draw guns as they frog-march me away.* I scream and wake up, disturbing both Lotty and Yoshi, who mutter at me disagreeably before falling back to sleep.

Remnants of the frightful dream stay with me for hours, even when I'm safely inside The Bell Chime, drinking a bowl of Chinese tea as I clean and mend a watch.

But the dream shouldn't have come as a surprise to me. Since we've all been confined to the ghetto, I've been searching for Mameh again. She's almost constantly on my mind. She must be here somewhere, in one serpentine alley or another. If she moved to the French Concession or the Settlement, she'd have been forced back to Hongkew by the Japanese to endure captivity with the rest of us Jews. I imagine myself meeting her by accident. She throws her arms around me, apologizing for her foolish and neglectful actions. She kisses and hugs me, asks how Lotty is, and comes back to the *heim* to live with us. I've already glimpsed women that I fantasize into Mameh as they hurry up the street and disappear into alleyways before I can catch up with them. Yesterday, the woman in front of me on Ward Street looked just like her — from the back, anyhow. As I tugged at her sleeve and she turned, I realized she wasn't my mother after all, but someone I'd never seen before.

"I'm so sorry," I said, "I thought you were somebody I knew."

"Obviously," she replied with a scowl, taking out her handkerchief and using it to wipe her sleeve, as though she thought I'd I'd contaminated it.

But today, as I leave The Bell Chime and am on my way to find Izo, because I haven't heard from her recently, I do catch sight of Mameh, my real Mameh, not a copy of her. She's standing on the other side of the crowded road dressed in a Persian lamb coat and wearing large emerald earrings. She must be living in luxury, must have found a rich man to take care of her.

"Mameh," I call. "Where have you been all this time?" I start to cross, weaving between bicycles and rickshaws in my hurry to greet her and implore her to come home.

I've now caught up with her, and we are facing each other. I half expect us to hold our hands out, one to the other, as in my dream. Instead, after glaring at me for a moment, she mutters one word, "Idiot."

A dark flush spreads from her neck to her forehead, and I notice beads of sweat breaking out on her mottled cheeks as if she's cornered. She draws the collar of her fur coat up, as though by doing so she can disguise herself, pretend to be somebody else. She doesn't ask how we are or how we're getting on without her. She just turns on her heel and melts into the flood of Jews and Chinese and vanishes. It's as though she's been swept away by the Whangpoo River, as though she's drowned. She recognized me, though, which I suppose is something, even though her one-word response was negative.

Instead of upsetting me, the sight of her frees me. It's as if an oppressive burden has been lifted from my shoulders and I can stand up straight again. I'm not going to waste any more tears on her. I was willing to forgive Mameh, but apparently she doesn't feel she's done anything that requires forgiveness. She doesn't want to be with us, was perhaps reluctant to tell her boyfriend she had children because he might throw her over. Now, after months of anxiety, of wondering miserably where she could be and whether she'd been killed, I don't want to be with her either. She's the idiot.

I finish my walk to the school, where I hope to intercept Izo. Lotty sees me first and canters over for a hug before starting back to the *heim*. When Izo appears, she looks grieved and downcast, not like her usual self at all. She begins to speak in a low, sad voice, telling me her mother has died and she is now all alone in the world.

"Not if I can help it," I say. "I lost my mother today too, although not to death. You are going to be Lotty's and my best friend no matter what happens, and we'll all be sisters."

CHAPTER 32

Herr Rubin and his wife, who stays in the flat upstairs, are both generous and warm. His wife, who asks me to call her Hunya, makes lunch for Herr Rubin and me every day, and suggests I bring my sister when she's not in school, so she can eat with us too. The Rubins have no children of their own and are becoming like parents to us. Herr Rubin has asked me to call him by his first name, Moshe. After hearing about Yoshi, the Rubins invite him to come to the shop, and Hunya feeds him as well. We're becoming quite a crowd. Sometimes, when she's not too depressed, Izo joins us, and I make sure to bring a loaf of bread or some little white fish that taste like pickled herring, or even one or two wonderful Viennese pastries, bought out of my salary. We cut them up so there's a morsel for everyone, including Song when he feels comfortable enough to visit.

"You don't need to do that," Hunya tells me. "You don't need to bring food." But I insist. Caring though they are, the Rubins can't be expected to feed the ravening hordes that constitute my adoptive family. The League of Nations, Yoshi calls it.

After lunch, Lotty usually stays upstairs with Hunya, who feeds her little bits of cakes and cookies all day long, dropping them into her mouth as if she's a baby bird rather than an eight-year-old and admonishing her to chew carefully. She tells my sister folk stories and teaches her different dances and songs from what she calls "the old country." Lotty loves performing them for Moshe, me, and any stray customers who wander into the shop.

As Moshe and I fix and clean watches, or wait for customers, we chat. He tells me about his brothers and sisters, all missing now, and I speak about my own family, telling him how I think about Tateh often, wondering if he's still alive, but I'm losing faith that he will ever return from the death camps.

"Don't lose hope, *maidel*. Things are changing. The tide has turned against the Nazis. They are losing their battles, both in the air and on the ground. Hitler is getting desperate and has called up children to fight because so many of his adult soldiers have been killed by our allies. Many of us believe that the war will soon be over, and those Jews still living, wherever they are, will be free again. Perhaps your Tateh will be a survivor," says Moshe, his back to me as he polishes a tall case clock. "Have faith. He might turn up as soon as the war ends."

"It's too late. He's been gone too long."

"He sounds like the kind of man who can beat all odds, your Tateh. And he's a clock enthusiast. That can't be bad. Why, somebody turned up in Shanghai a week ago who had escaped from Auschwitz." He smiles sadly, probably wondering if any of his own family will emerge alive from the ashes of war-torn Europe after the Nazis are vanquished.

I hesitate before murmuring, "I guess Tateh could be alive after all."

"Hold onto that possibility, Freda. It will keep you strong."

WITH FEARFUL BRAVERY ⎯⎯ 157

I try. But there's too much misery in Shanghai for me to feel much except my own powerlessness, my inability to help, though both Yoshi and I are doing what we can to assist the Underground after our last disastrous attempt.

Yoshi uses the rickshaw to convey disguised allies to safe houses when he can, providing *kipas* for the men and head-scarves for the women so they look Jewish. I deliver important packages on my way to or from work. I don't know what's inside their wrappings, just know they're coded, and I have to learn the addresses off by heart in case the Japanese stop me. Yoshi and I are both in terrible danger, would both be killed if caught. But the decapitation of the old man on the street was the tipping point for me after so many needless deaths, including, most recently, that of Izo's mother. What we're doing in the JJRS makes me feel useful, helps me from diving into a despair so deep I might never be able to climb out of it.

But even a thousand messages from a thousand members of the Underground can't dispel my dismay altogether, my torment. I blurt out to Izo one day how much I miss Tateh, especially now, as times are so bad. "He has woven himself into the fabric of my dreams, as he is killed over and over," I tell her. "I often wake up with my heart going full throttle."

"I do understand. I miss Mamma the way you miss your Tateh. I have a deep longing to see her again, though I've not missed my own father *for a single second*," she says, the words exploding out of her mouth. "Not since the moment the Nazis took him away. I don't care if he's dead. He was a brute to Mamma and us children. A big, vicious brute, always yelling and punching Mamma and my brother."

"I'm so sorry, Izo. I had no idea."

"I don't usually speak of it because it pales next to what others are experiencing. But it still stings. My father hit me too, often with a closed fist. He said it would make me behave. It didn't. It made me far worse, more angry and rebellious every time he did it. It made me fight back, clawing and kicking, though I was too little to do him much damage. But it also taught me how to look after myself. I didn't want to grow up to be like Mamma, who was timid as a mouse. He broke her spirit."

I don't know what to say, so I hug her instead. I'm upset she's not confided this to me before. But I'm holding something back too. A letter has arrived from Tateh via the Jewish Agency. As with the first missive, it has taken a long time to reach us, and is muddy, creased, and torn at the edges. But at least this time the woman from the Jewish Agency knew where to find us.

Dearest Malka, Freda, and Annalotte,

I think and worry about you often, hope that you're all well and happy. I've managed to survive so far, as I was strong from lifting tall case clocks when I arrived, and so have been kept alive to work, though my strength is waning. Tomorrow some of us workers are being trucked to another camp. If I have the opportunity, I'll drop this note from the truck as I go, and hope some kind person, a Polish farmer perhaps, will pick it up and forward it to the Jewish Agency. And then they may track you down. I don't know if I'll survive the move, and even if I do, I don't know what will happen to me afterwards. I long to see your dear faces, but have a presentiment that death might take me soon after I finish this letter.

Love to all of you, my dear ones,
Shmuel

I don't know whether to laugh or cry. He might still be alive. On the other hand, he might have died right after writing the note. Poor Tateh. I keep what he's written to myself, partly because if Lotty were to read it she'd take conjecture as fact, but also because, somewhat selfishly, I need to treasure it, keep it close to me. It gives me a faint flicker of hope, as delicate as the first tiny flame of a bonfire, blown by its maker into existence. It could so easily be extinguished in the same way that Izo's mother's life was. I tuck the note into a pouch, wearing it on a string around my neck — under my clothes and close to my heart — like an amulet. I can't bear the thought of losing it or sharing it with anyone. I hate the thought of its being passed from one hand to another, begin to hold the strange conviction that luck is somehow involved, that Tateh will remain alive as long as I keep the note safe.

CHAPTER 33

"Freda?"

"Yes, Lotty?"

"I'm starving. Is there anything to eat?"

"No, Lotty. You ask the same question over and over, and I always give you the same answer. You'll get something later."

Our lives, poverty stricken before, are now even meaner. Food is scarce, the value of my savings has dropped like a stone, the bank is still withholding our money, and our clothes are quite literally falling apart.

"My shirt has more holes than fabric," remarks Yoshi. "It looks like it's made of cobwebs." He whoops, startling Lotty, before scuttling sideways, spider-fashion.

We are still luckier than many, as both Yoshi and I are working and the Rubins are generous, though their money and stores of food are vanishing, as Hunya says, into the ether.

"Not surprising with all us monkeys around," I say, vowing to myself that I'll bring her more food as soon as I can.

"They 'have melted into air, into thin air,'" remarks the irrepressible Yoshi.

"Who have?" Lotty demands, biting her nails.

"Not who, what. Hunya's stores of food have."

"Is the 'melted into air' quote from *King Lear*?" I ask.

"No. Prospero. *The Tempest*." He grins at having bested me. But his grin resembles a rictus. Bony as a brontosaurus skeleton, his face ashy again, I grieve for him, though he's still alive. With liver and red meat scarce, it can't be for long.

He still beams, still laughs, still produces Chinese candies from his sleeve or pocket when they're available at the market. He still lights sparklers when he can get them. I think he does so in an attempt to comfort us; however, our situation is frightful and getting worse. He and I both know a candy or a card trick can't make things any better. Many refugees are thin as sticks and huddle in the *heim* in burlap bags, their clothing having completely disintegrated. Even Izo is skinny.

I tremble most for Song. He refuses to come in the *heim* or eat a share of what we have. He still sleeps on the street, no matter how bitter the weather. And the cold is savage in winter, the death rate accelerating as the thermometer plummets. His life is hanging on a precarious thread.

When we go to bed, Yoshi and I cuddle up in the same cot, with Lotty and the remnants of her dolly Mimi between us. I don't bother about respectability any longer. We need to keep warm. Our situation is far too serious to worry about appearances. Our neighbour in the next cubicle can tsk-tsk or spit on our curtain as often as she wants to. We're too busy trying to stay alive to pay her any mind.

Every day I touch Lotty's forehead to make sure she's not feverish. I begin to keep her away from school for fear of contagion, and she spends her days in the Rubins' flat, or the robin's nest, as she calls it, while I'm working downstairs. For the most part there are no visitors in the flat so she's safer, at least in the mornings. Deadly sicknesses — smallpox, scarlet fever, dysentery — to name only three of many — are everywhere. Often the refugees don't have the remedies or the stamina to recover from them.

So many have died that the corpses of Jews and others are stacked high in the streets. I'm reminded of Berlin, turn my face away till they're collected and buried. Sometimes, though, the earth is too freezing to welcome them and so they have to be cremated, which, although unavoidable, is against Jewish law. Will there never be an end to this blight? I cannot help but remember the Passover *seder*, with its catalogue of the plagues visited on the Egyptians. I pray that the war ends before our ashes, like those of the dead in Shanghai or the Jews in concentration camps, are swept away on the wind.

CHAPTER 34

At Chanukah, we give one another rain checks for gifts, vowing we'll replace them with real presents as soon as we can. I'll give Lotty a new doll and corking set, will present Izo with hot curling irons so she can marcel wave her hair, and will find a magic wand and book of spells for Yoshi. The only real gift I give is to Song. It's a long, wide scarf I knitted from scraps of wool so I can kid myself that if he wears it, he won't freeze to death. His warmth matters more to me than the inevitable blisters on my hands. He seems delighted, ties it around his high hat and casts both ends over his shoulders so that he resembles a Jewish man wearing a fringed prayer shawl.

In the evening, I suddenly remember New Oma's gold and silver brooch and take it from under the mattress to present to Lotty. "I'm deliriously happy!" she whoops, without a single stammer. She plays with the little stars for hours.

1945

The Year of the Cockerel

CHAPTER 35

S oon after, we usher in the new year. "Next year in Jerusalem," we all say to one another, as if it's Passover. Song,
who for once has been enticed inside by a piece of apple strudel,
repeats what we say correctly, though he has no idea what the
saying means. Every moment he's in the *heim*, he keeps watch
at the window to make sure no one steals the rickshaw.

A couple of months later, as I'm walking to The Bell Chime
on a sun-drenched winter's day, a shadow falls across the road.
I look up. A plane is flying by, so low that it barely misses
scraping the rooftops. It appears to be in slow motion. Eerily,
it's silent, and if it weren't for the shadow it casts, I'd never have
known it was there.

The plane's quiet presence is disconcerting, even sinister,
although there can be no doubt that it's American. So I should
be jumping with joy. After all, if an American aircraft can reach
Shanghai without being shot down, it's a wonderful predic-
tor that the Japanese and Nazis are becoming disorganized or
beaten back, that the war may soon end.

I have the uncanny, itchy sensation that if I stretch my arm way up I'll be able to touch the plane. The thought is downright scary. It jolts me into action. I tear across the road, hands over head, head down. After hiding in a doorway, my pulse banging erratically, I hear a soft whine as the plane gathers speed and altitude. After it's gone, I rush to tell the Rubins what I've experienced. I can't understand why the aircraft emitted no noise. Neither can they. And no customer coming into the store has noticed anything unusual.

Yoshi laughs aloud when I tell him what occurred. He's being very annoying; he sounds like a quacking duck. "The engines of planes make a tremendous racket as they fly by: Whoosh! Whir! Roar! They would fall out of the sky — Bang! Wallop! Smash! — if their ruckus stopped. You must have been dreaming."

"No, I wasn't," I say, deadly serious. "It was an omen, a sign, good or bad, of what's coming. I saw it with my own eyes."

"Of course, who else's eyes could you have seen it with?" he replies with his usual captivating grin, no doubt to mask his real feelings. Perhaps it's because he has become too afraid, as the war goose-steps on, to be optimistic. Later in the evening, by way of apology for his teasing, he offers to teach me Khanhoo, a game, he says, taught to him by a Chinese sage. I find it difficult to pick up. It uses more cards than a traditional pack, needs more concentration than I can muster right now.

"Let me play too," says Lotty. Yoshi adds even more cards to the pack and shuffles it with lightning fingers. Like me, Lotty hasn't a clue what's going on. We can't figure out the rules. So laying down his cards with éclat, Yoshi wins every hand. After an hour or so, he shouts out, "*Voilà*, I vin ze game."

At that moment the bombing starts in earnest. Lotty screams, and she's not the only one, I scream too, as do refugees all over the *heim*. There is nowhere to escape to. We have no bomb shelters.

CHAPTER 36

The bombs light up the sky as they drop. There are explosions all over Shanghai, except for Hongkew. So after the constant blare of sirens, the bombardment elsewhere in the city, the thundering and crashing, and the destruction that worsens each day, we finally realize that the Americans know who and where we are and deliberately avoid hitting us in their frequent raids. After that we hang out of windows or stand on roofs waving to the low fliers and yelling.

"Ja, ja!" shrieks Yoshi, almost falling out of the window in his enthusiasm. "The Americans have come to save us! We are going to win the war!"

In late spring we hear that the Nazis are defeated. The news is all over the local papers. For no longer than a second I picture Hans lying bloodied and dead in a battlefield. But his image soon fades, becomes transparent before vanishing as we dance and sing in the streets, joyful and triumphant. We are celebrating the death of that murderer Hitler and the arrest of his cronies. The festivities continue for days, interspersed with the roar of Japanese anti-aircraft guns and American bombs, which are still arrowing into other parts of the city.

If the Nazis are gone, can the Japanese be far behind? They show no signs of surrendering. The bombings continue each evening till almost the whole of Shanghai is ablaze. Smoke and dust sting our eyes and scorch our throats. And the summer heat, conflated with the fires, is all but unbearable.

I still go to work every day. I'll continue as long as the Rubins need me. One afternoon, while Moshe is upstairs, a young man enters. He looks vaguely familiar. After a moment I recognize who he is, although I've never seen him in civilian clothes before. He used to sit in the Green Lily with Hans and other Nazis, in full regalia, raucous and rude, yelling Nazi songs and drinking flagons of beer until he was half conscious. Now, divested of his companions and bravado, he creeps in timidly. I eye him with suspicion and an overwhelming sense of foreboding as he approaches the counter.

"Fräulein," he says, "I went to your home, but I was directed here by your sister."

"I see," I say, trying to sound noncommittal.

"I come here to tell you about your friend Hans."

"Yes?" I begin to shiver, anticipating what may come.

He hesitates. "I'm not sure how to say this. Why don't you sit down?"

"Can't you see there are no chairs here? Just spit out whatever it is you've come to say."

"I'm afraid I have bad news for you."

I was right then. *Something wicked this way comes.*

"Before he died ..."

My heart lurches and starts beating erratically. *"Died?"*

"Yes, Fräulein. You asked me to go on. I couldn't think of any gentler way to tell you. As I was saying, before he died, Hans wrote to me, asking me to let you know that he was about to be executed by the Führer, and he wanted to apologize to you for something he did. He told me he loved you."

Hans, with his honey eyes, his astonishing beauty, my best friend, my worst enemy, all stamped out? Hans, whose life was inexorably interwoven with mine?

"He entrusted me with this to give to you." The young man hands over a deeply creased photo of Hans and me playing together in the sandpit behind his house when we were very young. I can't believe that he kept the picture for so many years; he must have carried it around with him. He must really have cared for me. Even if he was betraying me with Opal, it doesn't matter now. *I forgive him for the trivial wrong he did me.* I can't speak. If I open my mouth, I'll scream.

"I'm so sorry. But you probably know he was secretly working against the Nazi party, and plotted to kill Hitler, as I ..." He tails off.

I'm too frozen to speak.

"The plot failed. He was hanged."

"*Hanged?*" I try not to believe it. I'm paralyzed, can't speak. There is a roaring in my ears, a stench of blood and decay.

"It was some time ago."

What does it matter when it was? It's not as though time could heal something that I didn't know about till now. It's as if it happened yesterday. Hans is dead. *He was hanged.* I can't imagine him not being in the world. I can't inhale. The earth stops rotating.

CHAPTER 37

Two days later the Americans begin to destroy Hongkew, thickly carpeting the entire area with bombs as they whiz by in their B12s. The sky is black with American aircraft. They look like enormous ravens, their powerful wings outspread as they glide and swoop. The ghetto is alight. Houses are flaming, shaking, crumbling. People, some of them on fire, shriek as they run through the streets. Jews and Chinese are killed as the bombs angle in. Cats and dogs lie hurt or dead on the road.

As soon as the all-clear sounds, we dash to help the injured. I warn Lotty to stay in the *heim*. Our corner is undamaged, so there's little risk to her inside. With all the falling masonry and threats of another air strike it's more dangerous for her to be out here with me.

Arms and legs stick out of the rubble. Chinese and Jews lie inert on the street. Yoshi and I try to lift the heaviest debris so we can get to those buried beneath. Others join us. Doctors have rushed in and are triaging the wounded before transporting the worst cases to hospital.

Suddenly I see one of the brightly coloured handles of Song's rickshaw protruding from a mess of bricks and stone. Dear God, he must be underneath, would have been sleeping beside or under the rickshaw as it's Yoshi's day off. Yoshi and I rush over, grab hold of the rickshaw handle, and pull. It breaks off. I see a corner of Song's scarf and pull on that too. It doesn't help. One of his forearms is sticking out, unmistakable because of his rickshaw uniform, and we pull on his hands till we realize how useless our efforts are.

Against orders, Lotty runs from the *heim* when she sees what we're doing. I suddenly realize with a shock that she can't be babied any longer. She's nine, going on ten. She and I grab Song's fingers and wrist and again try to wrestle him out. Izo runs from another pile of rubble to help us. No amount of pulling works, so we start to dig with our bare hands. I can hear Song crying below, and Yoshi calls back that he must be strong, that we will rescue him and give him a magic candy. He begins to tell Song jokes about rabbis and mandarins to keep his spirits up as we dig. None of us laugh.

Like the others, I'm desperate to rescue him and don't quit despite my overwhelming exhaustion and the headache from the knocks I received recently when I passed out and hit The Bell Chime's counter. But the stone is too heavy, the bricks too thick. We can't tunnel down to reach him though our nails are torn, our fingers bloody from trying. Gradually his crying subsides. I keep calling to him to hang on, we're almost there, he'll soon be out. Yoshi tells him a dreadful joke about a *yeshiva* boy and a coolie. Song doesn't respond. I try to take his pulse. He's dead.

Lotty throws herself on the pile of rubble and sobs uncontrollably. It's Izo who drags her away and attempts to comfort her.

"We did our best," whispers Yoshi, streams of tears making a patchwork of the earth and dust on his face. "It just wasn't enough. Bugger this stupid war." He kicks at a stone before running to try to assist another victim.

Izo takes Lotty back to the *heim*. She has grabbed his rickshaw handle and is cradling it. I sit in the middle of the road among heaps of rubbish, unable to speak or cry. The Americans are our allies. They did this after lulling us into the false belief that we were safe, that we were blanketed in security. Even if they didn't explicitly say that, we believed it. We cheered as we watched other parts of Shanghai explode and burn. Hundreds, perhaps thousands of Chinese civilians were sacrificed in order to annihilate the Japanese military in our region. I feel horribly ashamed that I laughed and clapped, that I waved as the Americans sliced the sky, bombing everything beneath except Hongkew. I hardly gave the victims of the raids a moment's thought. Now it's our turn. And now my innocent friend Song has become a victim too.

I sit by his cairn of stone and bricks for the rest of the day and through the night, although Yoshi tries to persuade me to leave. At dawn, as a sun red with smoke and dust rises above what's left of the buildings in Hongkew, I notice a group of five or six dogs of all colours and sizes picking their way through the devastation in single file. They pass by quietly, but keep turning their heads to look back. A thin, black mongrel comes into view. Terribly lame, wounded and bleeding, he limps after them. They keep stopping to wait for him to catch up before continuing to walk through the detritus. He's a member of their family, just as Song was a member of ours. I weep at their loyalty to one another.

Yoshi returns to remonstrate with me. Eventually I agree to leave the heap of rubble that's become Song's grave. Tortured with grief at his death as well as at the execution of Hans, whose murder I've scarcely had time to consider or mourn, I want to lament, howl, scream, but barely have the energy to whisper to Yoshi that I'm ready to go back to the *heim*.

CHAPTER 38

On September 2, my seventeenth birthday, blisteringly hot and slippery from sweat, I hurry through the familiar roads and alleys to The Bell Chime. People are running from their homes, crying and shouting on the streets. I can't tell whether they're happy or sad. Judging by what's been happening lately, it's probably another disaster somewhere, but I don't have time to ask them, as I'm so late for work.

Both Rubins meet me at the door of the shop.

"Sorry I'm late," I mutter. I've been late too many times over the past weeks, grieving for my friends and for people I didn't even know. I have to make a gargantuan effort just to push myself out of bed. For a few days after the raid in Hongkew I couldn't face getting up at all, I was too knotted up with despair to do anything except sleep. I would wake only long enough to remember the horrific mess that had become my life before falling asleep again.

"Really sorry," I say again.

But the Rubins are smiling. "Not a problem," says Moshe.

"We have a birthday present for you," says Hunya, grinning like the Cheshire cat in the English story about Alice.

"What is it?" I ask, my voice muted.

"The Japanese have surrendered! The war is over!"

I'm not sure whether to exult over the news or cry: I try to be pleased, but at the same time I'm horrified that the Americans dropped two atomic bombs on Nagasaki and Hiroshima in the days leading up to this surrender. Was it really necessary? The devastation must have been unimaginable. I've heard that thousands upon thousands of people — adults, children, and babies who were not warriors but ordinary civilians — were blotted out, leaving only their shadows on any walls that were still standing. In the past I would have felt jubilation, would have thrown my hands up and danced in triumph. But after witnessing the dreadful strikes on Hongkew and the rest of Shanghai, after seeing Song and so many others, even Germans like Hans, die so pitifully and needlessly, I'm shell-shocked, confused, cannot separate what's good from what's bad.

"Smile, Freda. It's a great day. We're free!" says Moshe, pouring wine for the three of us. "Happy birthday, *shaina maidel.*"

I smile mechanically. But although the senseless war might be over, it's left me, at least for the moment, with too many scars to celebrate.

CHAPTER 39

After having too little freedom for so long, we are now bewildered at having too much. The checkpoints are down, the Japanese have vanished, and we can wander the streets of Shanghai at will. I still have wages under my mattress, and more cash has been donated by one of the Jewish Agencies to resettle us. We are free to go anywhere in the world, but we still have no idea where that will be, and we don't know whether Izo wishes to accompany us. She has no one now but us. I ask her.

"That's what I wanted, but I didn't like to ask," she says. "I won't show you up. I'll wear my best clothes and spiky high heels."

I groan.

Hours later, with Izo joining us, we resume our discussion about where to go.

"Not Germany," I say.

"Definitely not Poland," says Yoshi.

"How about Hollywood?" suggests Izo. "I could be a film star. It's what I've always dreamed of."

We sit on the steps outside the *heim*, as the heat is even more torrid inside than it is here. Two American soldiers pass by, smiling as they toss us packets of gum and chocolate bars. I haven't tasted chocolate in ages. We all thank them.

"I'd rather have nylons." Izo sighs. "But chocolate is a good second choice."

"Canada is a fine place," I say as we enjoy the chocolate. "My father had a cousin in Montreal, Ben Isen. He's probably still there and will welcome us with open arms. I'm sure the Jewish Agency can find out his address. And there'll be specialists there, Yoshi, who can find out what's really wrong with you."

"There's nothing wrong with Yoshi," insists Lotty. "He picks me up and twirls me around."

"Even though you're so big?"

"Even so."

Yoshi grins.

"I'm sure we'll need visas," I continue. "The Canadians were turning Jews away during the war, but perhaps now it will be different. If we apply for immigration papers, we'll find out."

"I see you've got it all worked out," says Yoshi. "Have some chocolate, Lotty."

"You eat it. I have my own," she says. "But if there's any left over later, we can negotiate."

We all laugh.

CHAPTER 40

The next day we present ourselves for immigration papers.

"Immigration is very tight in Canada," an official tells us, staring at us through thick lenses that make his eyes into tiny darting fish. "I see that two of the young ladies have an uncle in Montreal, which should prove most helpful. We could help find his address if need be. But what about the other two?"

"Izo is like our sister. She will have no one if we leave without her. She has lived with us for a very long time — all through the war," I say. This is not, strictly speaking, a lie. Izo has slept in another cubicle in the same room as us since we arrived in Shanghai.

"Izo is my best friend. She's a great looker-afterer," adds Lotty.

"And the young man?"

"Freda and I are going to get married when we reach Montreal. I can't imagine life without her."

I try to hide my surprise, feel myself blushing. We haven't discussed marriage and neither of us is ready for it. I may never be ready for it, but have to admit that even if it is a lie, it's a pretty interesting one.

"I'll take it under advisement," says the official. Lotty looks blank. He smiles at her. "That means, young lady, that I'll let you know."

"Please make it fast," she begs.

On the way home we discuss our chances.

"You gave him the lie direct," I tell Yoshi.

"Oh, very good. Touchstone. *As You like It*," he replies. "You're almost a Shakespeare scholar. I hope the guy buys my story, which I borrowed from you. When we were looking for a flat, that is. I bet he will. He looks timid as a hummingbird in those enormous spectacles of his. In any case, I hope we do marry when we're older."

"I'll take it under advisement," I reply, smiling.

"If you don't marry Yoshi, I will," announces Lotty. "He gives me the best hugs and cuddles!"

Everyone grins. For the first time I feel a lightness, an almost-happiness and serenity I haven't experienced in years.

A month later we're moving out of the *heim*, our immigration papers in hand, Lotty's and my small cache of belongings in the shabby old suitcase that Mameh brought from Berlin so many years ago. The immigration official came through with cousin Ben's address, 5325 Hutchison Street, Montreal. I've sent him a letter to tell him we're coming.

We've said goodbye to Hunya and Moshe; we cried and hugged one another and ate a special farewell cheesecake that Hunya baked for the occasion. We took all our tin mugs, as well as those of Mameh, New Oma, and Izo's mother, and made a solemn procession to the park, where we hung them from the branches of a tree with bits of string. We held one another's hands as the mugs dangled in the wind, glinting in early sun.

"It's a cup tree," Lotty said with satisfaction.

"And it's a sign that we were here," replied Yoshi.

"And that we prevailed," I added solemnly.

"Enough of the sombre!" Izo rolled her eyes. "No need to get so dopey over a bunch of dented mugs."

The next day we're ready to quit the *heim* forever. "What about Tateh?" I cry suddenly, sitting back down on my cot.

"What about him?" asks Izo. Having painted her toenails crimson, she wiggles her feet into her peep-toed high heels.

"How can I leave? What if he turns up here?" Much missed, no doubt reinvented by me in the intervening years since I last saw him, he still is very sturdily a fixture in my world, the one missing person I'm hanging onto. I'm not yet willing to give him up.

"We'll send a forwarding address to the Jewish Agency," Yoshi replies, "if the immigration official hasn't already done so. Never fear. And if he's survived, he might just arrive at Ben's before we do, so that's something to hope for. Now get a move on or we'll miss the boat."

"Just a moment," I say as we go through the door. I drop the suitcase and face the *heim* as if it's the Wailing Wall of Jerusalem. This is where Song and New Oma died. Izo's mother died here too. Close by is the Green Lily Café, where I renewed and lost my romantic friendship with Hans. I lean my forehead against the wall and say silent goodbyes to all of them. If it weren't for the war they might still be alive, but at the same time, if it weren't for the war, I'd never have met Song or New Oma, or come across Hans for the second time. *I forgive him*, I reiterate silently, before murmuring a prayer for the dead and for those of us still living. It's my own Wailing Wall.

"Hurry up," my sister yells impatiently.

I turn to my little family, who are walking toward the harbour

— except for Yoshi, that is, who's performing cartwheels along the road after throwing his bundle of clothes and magic tricks over to Izo. She juggles them with her own packages before flashing her lipstickiest grin at him. "You should be in a circus," she says, giggling.

"We're about to sail to Canada! To a brave new world!" I shout.

Yoshi stops mid-somersault and falls, almost bashing his head on the pavement. "Miranda!" he shouts back. "*The Tempest*! Shakespeare!"

"Right!" I pick up the suitcase. "O brave new world, that has such people in't." I look at them all. They are *my* people. "Wait for me, guys. I'm coming."

ACKNOWLEDGEMENTS

I'd like to extend my thanks

To Marc Côté and Barry Jowett for accepting my novel, *With Fearful Bravery*;

To Barry Jowett for his thoughtful substantive edit, and his belief that the book was good enough to publish, which sustained me during the rewriting and editing of it;

To everyone else at Cormorant and Dancing Cat Books who gave good advice and participated in the line editing, advertising, printing and publicity of my novel;

To my dear agent Margaret Hart, who is about to leave HSW and go on to other life projects — I don't know what I'll do without her;

To my wonderful husband Michael and terrific son Adam, who both gave me suggestions and helped with the editing;

To my mum, who has read all my books, encouraged me in the writing of them, and plies me with cake, cookies and tea whenever I visit her;

To the rest of my supportive family including Jamie, my lovely daughter;

To all my friends, writerly, neighbourly and Shakespearean;

To the Canada Council of the Arts, whose extremely generous grant I used to finish this novel;

And to all my readers, wherever you are, a great big thank you!